Sundial

Dear Donna,
Thank you for your
continued support and
encouragement. It means
the world to me.
Blessings & love,
Jill Hicks

Jill Hicks

This book is a work of fiction. Names, characters, businesses, organizations, places, events, and incidents either are the product of the author's imagination or are used fictitiously. Any resemblance to actual persons, living or dead, or events is entirely coincidental.

Cover photograph and design by Bill Hicks

*This book is dedicated to
all who have pondered
the "what ifs" of life.*

CHAPTER ONE

FAITH
~ Recalling a day in 1978 ~

With my shorts down around my ankles, I sat perched upon the only toilet seat in my parents' small ranch house. In silence I stared at the little vial of liquid that I had placed, only minutes ago, on the vanity beside me. Unable to look away, I watched in horror as the vial's contents slowly turned pale blue.

"This can't be right! How could this have happened?" I shrieked from somewhere deep within my gut, making sure no sound escaped my lips. I couldn't risk giving up my hiding place, or my need for seclusion.

This just can't be right.

Trembling, I reached into the small trash basket on the other side of the commode, pulled out the instructions, and skimmed through them again.

Shit. Something's got to be wrong. Please, tell me this is wrong.

A more careful study confirmed what I already knew: I had performed the test exactly as directed.

Panic set in.

On the opposite side of the bathroom door, everyone else in the world was moving through their day as planned and at a pace they controlled. Inside my small confines, time was racing at breakneck speed. My impending damnation was playing out before me. Horrific scenarios ran helter-skelter through my head. I couldn't catch my breath. My chaotic thoughts dashed in every direction as I tried to come to grips with the result that had just materialized before my eyes. What I had feared for the past two months had been confirmed. A small amount of urine added to a test kit solution had just incriminated me. My indictment was no longer in question and my sentence would be levied in nine months' time. The waiting game was over. My anxious uncertainty had been replaced by visions of a frightening, ill-fated future.

My respiration accelerated, becoming shallower. I tried to think of possible ways to challenge the findings. To prove the science wrong. To save myself.

I thought back to the times my behavior could have played a role in the disastrous result.

What could I have done differently?

Several things came to mind.
Moments—very intimate and passionate moments—came to mind.

I thought we were being careful . . .

I stared at the vial again, hoping the blue solution would fade to clear.

Maybe it's a false positive . . .

There was no change, not even the slightest. The aftermath of my ineffective preventive measures—of which there were none—was sitting on the vanity, at eye level, staring back at me. Glaring at me. That little vial had just consumed my every hope of obtaining the joys that should come with adult independence.

That vial owned me.

My parents . . . they are going to kill me. They're going to be mad as hell. How am I going to tell them? Or anyone else, for that matter?

Noah . . . my God, Noah . . . look at what we've done.

And, how will Noah take this news?

Technically, I guess, he could just move on without me. Without "this." But I'll have no choice. I'll have to live with this for the rest of my life.

The responsibilities of all my remaining days came crashing down on me. The weight of reality sat heavy on my chest. My lungs were being compressed, as if strangled by a boa constrictor. I was finding it even more difficult to breathe.

And if my parents disown me, well, I could end up alone, and with a newborn.
End of story.

This is the end of my life as I know it, or as I thought it would be.

I felt dizzy. My temples throbbed.

What am I going to do? I can't believe this. I'm a good girl. I really am. Things like this shouldn't happen to people like me.

My older sister is going to have a field day. There will be no sympathy from her. She'll tell me how stupid I am. I can hear her now, "Haven't you two heard of condoms? Only an idiot gets pregnant at seventeen!"
She will skip through life and I will have to watch her live happily ever after while I become a single mother, probably living in poverty. She will flaunt the lifestyle I will

never have: the right way to do things, the order in which young ladies are meant to grow up and find happiness.

Seventeen, almost eighteen.

Does this mean my parents could have Noah arrested and charged?
No. They can't. I won't let them. Dear God, don't let that happen.

The thought of Noah and me being ripped apart was more than I could bear, but it was inevitable now.

Tears began flowing steadily down my cheeks as my shoulders heaved in distress. I leaned over my knees, and closed my eyes.

He can't leave me. God, don't let him leave me . . .

Isolated in the bathroom, I was having my very own personal crisis all because of a stupid home pregnancy kit that I had purchased at the drugstore. I sat there, guilty and ashamed, dreaming up the worst that could happen to me. My feet and legs fell asleep due to the lack of circulation.

Finally, with all the stale oxygen having been sucked out of that claustrophobic bathroom, I carefully dumped the solution down the drain, rinsed out the vial in order to thoroughly dispose of the test results, and then slid the kit back into the box with the directions and disclaimers. I placed the box and its contents back into the little white pharmacy bag.

For now, I will have to hide the truth. No one can know. Not yet, anyway.

My plan was to slip out the back door and throw the remaining evidence into the trash container around the side of the house where no one would find it. In two days, it would be buried in a landfill, but the outcome of my actions would be growing inside me. In several months' time, I would be showing. The rumors would start and intensify. I would begin the death sentence levied upon the life that was slipping away from me.

I put the white paper bag on the vanity and rose from the toilet seat. My legs and feet pulsated and stung as blood began to flow unobstructed to and from my toes.

This is it. It's over. As soon as I step outside this door, nothing will ever be the same again.

The house was eerily still; as if it knew that I was a "dead man walking." I moved with stealth-like caution, hoping not to be noticed.

After depositing the bag and its contents into the trash receptacle outside, my first instinct was to go down to the river and contemplate my next steps. Sitting on the dock, alone, had always been my sanctuary. Now, more than ever, I needed to seek the calming effect of meditating in solitude over the water. First, though, I took a slight detour to my bedroom and grabbed a shell that Noah had given me almost a year before. I had high hopes that it would bring me the comfort that he had promised it would.

As I tried to rest with my eyes closed and my face to the sun, my conscience demanded that I replay all the times conception could have taken place. For my own sanity, I needed to pinpoint the exact moment the guilty sperm had been released into fertile ground and its hunt began. I wanted to know when the microscopic tadpole had intercepted its intended target. I supposed it would make me feel better if I could pinpoint a specific lapse in judgment. A way to lay blame. How strange is that? It's just that I thought we had been careful. Very careful. However, deep down, I think I knew all along when it had happened. It was probably the one time Noah did more than just dabble on the edge. Before that night, he had always exhibited an enormous amount of restraint. No matter how hard I had tried to pull him in, he always resisted my irrepressible desire for full penetration. It was the one time he had surprised me by responding to my desperate demands to have all of him. Dare I admit that it was my first time to go that far? And, as I found out later, it was his first time, too. Unprepared, we had gone farther than we had obviously anticipated. I remember reveling in the sensation of our oneness when suddenly Noah sharply inhaled and then let out a hefty groan. Quickly, he rose from me, moaning and letting loose a hot torrent on the inside of my thigh.

"Dear God . . . Oh, Faith, I. Am. So. Sorry."

Noah's body shook and jerked as he moaned one last time before collapsing on top of me. Rolling over, he scrambled to grab his T-shirt that had been discarded earlier on the boathouse floor.

"Here, use this," he had the wherewithal to direct.

On the cusp of potentially my first intercourse-induced orgasm, my body was rendered helpless. Reeling and breathless, I unconsciously took the T-shirt from his hand. I had been left hanging on the precipice of a stratosphere that I had never climbed before. I wanted more. I wasn't ready to come down without falling over the summit that I had just ascended with such strong determination. But already, the fluid on my soft skin was cooling.

Coming down from the cliff, I bundled Noah's T-shirt in my hand and began wiping my inner thigh to remove the outpouring of our unplanned consummation.

"I think I pulled out in time," Noah panted huskily, as he pulled his briefs back on, his shoulders now glowing with perspiration in the moonlight that was peering through the single window of my father's boathouse.

After I finished cleaning up, I handed the soiled T-shirt back to Noah. He stood and quietly walked out onto the dock.

While gathering myself, and dressing, I watched him as he leaned over the edge of the dock and swooshed his T-shirt back and forth through the water of the dark silvery river.

Wringing out his shirt, Noah returned and leaned against the doorframe.

"I'm so sorry, Faith. Are you OK?"

"I'm fine. Come back in, please, and hold me."

Two months and several weeks later, in the summer of 1978, I was almost eighteen and I had just learned that I was undeniably pregnant. Noah and I were just two years into our relationship.

In that second year, we *had* fantasized about a possible future together. In letters, we had shared our adolescent ideas about adult life such as marriage, kids, what type of dog we'd have, and where we'd build our house. It makes me laugh now to think that we were able to fantasize about such responsibilities, yet we were too uncomfortable to talk about the inevitable if we didn't take precautions. And *if* we were going to have full-blown sex, then we should have considered some form of birth control or contraception.

I blame myself. I was the impatient one.

Before that, everything had been rosy because we were, after all, just kids still living under the roofs of our parents' homes. We had been securely cocooned by their protection . . . or so we had thought. In the heat of that night, in a cozy boathouse, there was no one there to protect us from ourselves.

I had been terribly naïve about many things, and found myself pregnant. And through it all, I had never seen Noah's naked body. Everything had always taken place under a sheet or a blanket, mostly because I was too embarrassed about my own body, especially below the waist. Indeed, when studying my reflection in the mirror, I would observe—and even admire—the changes in my breasts, but never really wanted to know what was happening south of my belly button. So, during our times of intimacy, I always wanted to be covered up. I loved his touch, and I know he enjoyed the feel of my skin. And though he had seen me from the waist up, I had never taken a gander at him from the waist down. I was afraid that if I took a curious peek, I would not be able to stop staring, wanting to study the matter further. Then, he would catch me gawking and think I was some kind of immature weirdo. I guess it was some sort of misguided respect . . . maybe.

Years later, I learned differently. Men like it when you look. My husband, Tyler, knows every inch of my body, and I have memorized his in every condition and state of grandeur. Now, I cringe when I think about all the misgivings of my awkward youth.

In 1978, when I told Noah about my unexpected expectancy, he didn't believe me, at first.

"Are you sure? We've been careful. I've been *very* careful. How did this happen?" he asked incredulously, rubbing his forehead with his long slender fingers.

"I don't know. I mean . . ."

I wanted to remind him of the boathouse event—the one where he believed he had pulled out in time—but I was afraid to imply that it was entirely his fault.

"I'm not sure. All I know is that the test said I'm pregnant."

Noah was a good guy. He really was. I know, everyone says that about their first pass at love. But Noah was an exceptional young man. He would have done anything for me no matter the selfless sacrifice required of him. (Something I had lost sight of in my state of panic in the bathroom with the damning vial of unwanted news.)

Noah also had a bright future ahead of him. He was a brainiac and due to leave that fall for his freshman year at Boston University, and grant it, I was already distraught about his attending a school that was a full day's drive away. Once he left, I would only see him during term breaks and holidays, if he came back at all. Even before the confirmation of my condition, I was beginning to feel abandoned.

Everything had been turned upside down and inside out. I had no idea what life would look like in nine months' time, or any day thereafter.

That was sixteen years ago. Now I am thirty-three, almost thirty-four, and married with two young daughters.

CHAPTER TWO

NOAH

~ May 1994 ~
Sixteen years later

It was a beautiful Sunday morning. The church was filled with the usual suspects and there was a heightened air of excitement in the sanctuary. Perhaps it was the anticipation of scheduled events everyone had planned for the afternoon. The temperature was predicted to reach a high of eighty-four degrees. It was going to be the type of spring day when grills would be uncovered for the first time since the previous fall and the supermarket shelves would be emptied of hamburger rolls and potato salad. The boat ramps would be stacked up as weekend captains waited for a space to launch their vessels. Boatyards would be abuzz with owners returning to wax hulls and provision their yachts. Every retail ice chest in Cecil County, Maryland, would be emptied out by early afternoon. Even I felt the desire to wrap it up quickly so Chrissy and I could get on with the rest of our day.

I had just concluded my sermon and, as always, I ended the service with a prayer. That's when I heard a familiar utterance from somewhere amongst the congregation of nearly two hundred people.

"Show's over. Can we go now?"

A reflexive lump caught in my throat. I looked up from the pulpit.

I know that voice . . .

I strained to see her as I robotically pronounced my final words: "Now, go in peace."

Frozen in place as the organist played the introduction to the closing hymn, I feverishly scanned the sanctuary looking for her. The music and singing throughout the small chapel began to swell and swirl, homogenizing in the rafters of the high ceiling.

"Be Thou my vision, O Lord of my heart
Naught be all else to me, save that Thou art"

I chuckled silently. The irony of the first line was not lost on me. Staying in the pulpit, above the congregation, I had a better chance of locating her. I was determined to find her.

There . . .

She stood, helped her mother to her feet, grabbed her mother's jacket and purse, and then glanced back at me with an uncertain look on her face. Slowly, she and her mother, who was a regular parishioner at my church, made their way to the back. They were the first to exit through the double stained glass doors, now appropriately propped open.

I took a deep breath.

Obviously in town for a visit, Faith Cuthbertson Livingston's presence would haunt me for the remainder of the day.

Is this a weekend visit?
What are the chances that I'll run into her while she's here?
That would be awkward.

It might surprise you to know that although I am a pastor, I am, nonetheless, a man full of many self-doubts. Whether I'm standing behind the pulpit, receiving parishioners at the door, or having a serendipitous meeting with a congregant in the supermarket, I am always "on," concerned with how I might be perceived. It's the feeling that one is being watched, always under the microscope, all the time, and it's exhausting.

Praise God for Chrissy, my wife of eight years. She is my earthly counselor and best friend. I can always be myself around her. She is my sounding board, my chief editor, critic, and my confidante. Usually, our ride home from church is replete with a survey of my morning's work.

"How was my message?"
"Do you think I got the point across?"
"Did I ramble on too long?"

In her critiques, Chrissy, in her own tactful way would first list the positive aspects of the morning's message before launching into anything that "could have been better." However, that morning was different.

"It was a wonderful service, Noah. Now, can we please enjoy the rest of our day?"

We traveled the newly-resurfaced Route 272 in silence. Lost in my thoughts, and overwhelmed by the vapors coming from the heated asphalt, I almost allowed Chrissy's indifference to go unnoticed.

CHRISSY

I knew who she was. Her mother had been a member of the church long before Noah had arrived as the senior pastor. Yet, on that day, several of my friends, members of my women's Bible study, had found it necessary to scoot up next to me and point her out during Noah's closing prayer. Rumor had it that she had returned to care for her widowed mother who was recovering from a nasty fall.

Noah, my husband, had performed the memorial service for her father about nine years earlier. (Noah and I had begun dating at about the same time.) Afterward, many had speculated that Mrs. Cuthbertson, the mother, might move to Seattle to be with her youngest daughter, Faith, Faith's "very successful" husband, and their two children. Noah had even mentioned in passing that he would miss Mrs. Cuthbertson if that were to happen. He was fond of the lady who had always been like a second mother to him.

To date, nothing about the Cuthbertsons had really affected me. I knew about Noah's high school sweetheart. I saw her mother almost every Sunday, and she was a dear woman who always acknowledged me and told me how blessed I was to have landed such a kind and Godly man. But that particular morning, I saw how shocked Noah was to see the youngest Cuthbertson daughter, who just happened to be his first love.

I felt the stirring of Noah's soul when she rose from her pew. There wasn't much that Noah and I could hide from each other. At least that's what I needed to believe.

FAITH

When it came to personal or sensitive subjects, my mother was a woman of few words. She never volunteered much information about her past, including her medical history, which mothers should share with their daughters. I always had to carefully extract such private details with kid gloves. Holding a conversation with my mother about such things was much like an archeological dig. *Careful, careful . . . dust it off and circle around it carefully.* In return, she never asked about my own present ups and downs. Perhaps that explains why I had been so uncomfortable discussing intimate matters, like birth control, with Noah.

Growing up, life could be so confusing and lonely at times in our silent household. It probably explains my many adolescent hours spent on the dock, alone with my thoughts, and away from everyone else. There, I would occupy myself searching for cerebral answers to life's mysteries by observing Mother Nature's behaviors. I was particularly interested in her repetitive, rhythmic patterns, and the surrounding chaos that potentially threatened her delicate balance.

My father wasn't home much of the time because he had to work long hours to support my mom, my older sister, and me. Dad owned a hardware store on South Main Street in the small town of North East, Maryland. The town was named after the river upon which it is situated. The area is also known as "The Head of the Chesapeake Bay," which is quite unfitting for such an enchanting little village. In actuality, its moniker is solely attributed to its relative location and its importance to the Bay.

Dad was always up early in the morning to open his store for the local contractors and watermen, and home late in the evening after finishing his orders and payroll. Many nights I would be headed off to bed while he was just sitting down at the kitchen table to eat his reheated dinner beneath the harsh glow of one bleak suspended light fixture. He looked much older with the direct, unmuted illumination casting deep shadows beneath his tired and drooping facial features.

"Good night, Daddy. I'll see you in the morning."

"Lord willing and the creek don't rise," he would always respond.

I never knew why Dad bothered to refer to the Lord in any way. My father never went to church. Sundays were a big day at the store with all the weekenders coming through town. However, my mother could be found in the old chapel every Sunday morning, sitting in her favorite pew. When we were younger, she would drag my older sister and me off to Sunday school. In a tiny room in the back of the red brick building, our class would sing our little songs, color in our workbooks, and make a craft usually involving cutout paper dolls dressed like shepherds on popsicle sticks. We were taught that God loved us and that we should always be good. We were even given a list of ten things we had to promise not to do in order to be considered "good enough." They were the "Thou Shalt Nots." Honestly, at the time, I didn't even know what half of them meant. But if I was found guilty of any one of those "Shalt Nots," apparently there was a place for me—and all of the other bad children like me—to go after I died, as if the thought of dying wasn't already scary enough. All those sinners piled up on top of one another somewhere below the surface of the earth where it was very hot. Hot lava, swirling around everywhere . . . they were down there screaming and "gnashing their teeth." It sounded pretty horrifying to me.

However, in my youth, I was only worried about such things on Sunday. By Monday morning, I was on my way back to school or out to play in the summer sun on our narrow stretch of beach. Besides, I was fairly certain that I was in better steads with God than most of my peers. If not, I figured I had a lot of years left to straighten things out with the "Big Man in the Sky." Even still, I always had the feeling that He was up there looking down on me, just waiting for me to screw up.

How was I to know that just before reaching adulthood, I would really mess up . . . all because I had committed one of the deadly "Thou Shalt Nots."

NOAH

I remember how I felt, as though it were yesterday. There was no official date or deliberate declaration of a breakup. She never said, "I'm sorry, but . . ." and I never asked, "What's wrong?"

We just fell apart.

In 1978, several weeks prior to departing for my freshman year at Boston University, our relationship took a steep nosedive. I was going to spend the weekend on my parents' yacht, the "Nauti-Lass," which they kept docked at Bay Boat Works, in North East, Maryland. On my way through town, I had planned to pick up Faith from her part-time job at a local diner and we would spend a quiet evening on my parents' yacht, just the two of us. My parents weren't due to come down until the next day. (We lived forty-five miles away in West Chester, Pennsylvania, which is located approximately twenty-five miles southwest of Philadelphia.) Faith had an eleven o'clock curfew, but at least we would have several hours to ourselves.

Faith and I had met two years earlier, during the summer of 1976. She lived just on the other side of North East.

The first time I had ever laid eyes on Faith, I was at the North East Firemen's Carnival, just strolling around the grounds. I had nothing better to do that night. It was then that a young lady, about my age, caught my eye. It wasn't her striking appearance that got my attention. Faith was sort of a tomboyish, plain-Jane type, which I later found very charming. Rather, it was her laugh and bright smile that reeled me in.

Faith was volunteering at her church's water ice stand, helping some very young children with their frozen sugary concoctions. When one of the toddlers was accidently shoved by a passer-by in a big hurry, Faith reached out to save the little girl and a cardboard tray of water ice from hitting the dusty ground. She was successful with the exception of one casualty: Faith's apron. The tray of water ice flew up against the white linen fabric and left large colorful polka dots of cherry red and blueberry blue across her midriff. Faith looked down at her apron and began laughing. "Well, look at this piece of artwork!" she chuckled. "I couldn't have done better if I tried! And for you," she said, looking at the pouting little girl, "you can have all the water ice you want for the rest of the night!" The little girl, who was just about to break into wailing hysteria, was now jumping up and down and clapping. It was truly very sweet. There was such an innocence and playfulness about Faith that I was immediately drawn to her. She was the kind of person one wanted to be around.

I didn't see Faith again until several weeks later when I was out on the Nauti-Lass with my parents and younger brother. It was the end of the day and we were cruising up the channel of the North East River when I noticed a small sailboat tipped over. Only the bottom of the hull was visible through the intense sunset glare coming off the water. I yelled to my father and pointed out the small craft that appeared to be in distress. He pulled up within thirty feet of the little vessel and, much to my dad's dismay, I went overboard and swam out to it. As soon as I put my hand on the overturned hull, I recognized the young lady with drenched hair. She was none other than the same one who had been volunteering at the carnival donning the sacrificial apron.

"Could you use some assistance?" I asked.

A quick study of the situation and I could see that she was all right. She was wearing the same exuberant smile and her voice had that happy-go-lucky lilt.

"That would be great! She turtled this time and I'm having some trouble getting her righted."

"OK. Stay put. Let me see if the mast is stuck in the bottom."

"That's not necessary. It's fine. I already checked."

Admittedly, I was surprised. This girl knew what she was doing. I looked up—way up—at my dad who was seated in the fly bridge of the Nauti-Lass, waiting to see if I knew what to do next.

"OK, let's get a line around the masthead and see if we can pull her up and over," I suggested.

"Sounds like a plan!" she agreed with the same enthusiasm she had demonstrated the first time I had laid eyes on her.

I yelled to my mom and asked her to grab a line from the stern locker and throw it out to me. She and my younger brother were standing at the rail watching. My mother gathered a line and heaved the running end in my direction with good accuracy.

"Be careful!" my mom called out, because that's what mothers do.

I caught the running end of the line and Mom looped the spliced end around the stern cleat of the Nauti-lass. With everything ready, I dove under the water to find the masthead. It was a little tougher than I had thought it would be because the fully submerged sail tried to swallow me. I had to resurface, take a second breath, and try again. The third time was the charm. Everything secured, the young lady and I swam away from the little sailboat to avoid being hit by the mast or the boom, in case they suddenly popped up. I circled my arm in the air, signaling my Dad to slowly throttle forward. As the Nauti-Lass's props started to turn, the little Tech Dinghy began rolling over. Once the masthead and sail appeared on the surface my dad stopped all forward motion. Now, the tricky part: I had to untie the line from the masthead while treading water. (I know, I should have had a lifejacket on. A maneuver my dad lectured me about later.) I managed to keep the masthead at the surface while wrangling the line loose. Lying on its side, the hull took on water. When ready, the dinghy's spry captain swam over to her boat, held on to its gunnel and leveraged all her weight—which wasn't much—onto the centerboard, popping the boat upright. Once the sail was free of water, the boom swung wildly. The sail luffed like an old decrepit dog trying to shed water from its heavy coat. The main sheet hung loose and thankfully untangled itself from the rudder. The cockpit was full of water.

"Don't worry, she won't sink," the vessel's very able captain said as if she had read my mind.

The little dinghy stood at attention with her sail luffing in the light breeze. Perfect.

"Looks good!" the young lady shouted. "Thank you so much! I could've been out here forever if you hadn't stopped."

"Or run over. It was difficult to see you in the sun's glare. Stay out of the channel from now on," I directed without realizing how preachy I sounded. (A foretelling, I'm sure. I should have known then.)

"Yes, Sir!" she saluted.

While I added my weight to the opposite side of the small boat, she agilely climbed over the gunnel and back into her tiny watercraft. It was as if we instinctively knew what to do to without saying a word. Seeing her come out of the water, I couldn't help but notice just how svelte she was—all muscle.

Filled with water, the dinghy had very little freeboard above the surface of the river. Her captain began bailing with a bucket tied to the mast.

This has happened before, I surmised.

"Do you need some help with that?" I asked.

"No, I just need to get this water out of here so she's stable enough to sail."

She bailed several more large buckets full.

"What's your name?" I asked, still hanging on to the Tech Dinghy while she continued to bail. My legs were getting tired.

"Faith."

"How far do you have to go, Faith?" I asked.

"Just other there."

She pointed to a rickety dock and dilapidated boathouse that were tucked back inside a small cove. The shoreline was covered in trees right down to the water's edge. A thin band of sand provided a narrow delineation between the property and the water.

"I'll be fine, now," she assured me as she began gathering the mainsheet in one hand and the tiller in the other.

I knew, then, it was time to push off or she was going to drag me into the cove with her.

"Thanks again!"

"You're welcome . . . anytime."

"Hopefully, there won't be a next time," she laughed. It was that same contagious lighthearted spirit that had attracted me weeks ago.

"Sure. Right," I responded, trying not to sound too disappointed.

"Well, show's over! Time to go!" she said looking straight at me. "Thank you!" she yelled, waving to my parents as the boat began to respond to the westerly breeze now filling out its sail.

"Anytime," my dad returned.

Faith sailed off, leaving me in the tiny wake of her little sailboat.

"Come on, Romeo," my dad lampooned, "before you drown."

"Did you see him save that girl?" my little brother cheered.

Two years later, in 1978, Faith quietly told me that she was pregnant.

I remember saying some really stupid things before I had noticed the tears floating in her eyes.

"I'm so sorry, Faith. I thought we were being careful. Are you sure about this?"

"All I know is that I'm late—very late—and the liquid in the kit turned blue, meaning I'm pregnant. I'm nauseous at night and I'm very tired during the day."

"Jesus, Faith, this changes everything."

"I'm so sorry, Noah."

"Don't apologize. It's not your fault. We're in this together, you and I. I love you, Faith. You know that, right? I've loved you since the first time I saw you. We're a team, Faith, and it's best we found out now. There's still time for me to change my plans. I'll take a year off and we can get married and I'll start school later, that's all."

"That's all? Our parents are going to flip! They'll be so mad. Nothing could be worse than this: unmarried and pregnant. And what about the baby? You think we can do this? Raise a child? Neither one of us has a steady job that could sustain us. And, where would we live?"

"I could ask my parents for financial help," I suggested hesitantly. Reality was beginning to insert itself into our situation.

"My mom might be able to help with babysitting, if we could stay in North East. Do you think that's possible? Could we find a place here?" Faith asked tentatively.

"I don't see why not."

"But this is crazy. You're supposed to leave for college."

"I'll delay it."

"Noah, things will get so crazy with a baby and work, you won't have a chance to go back to school or even get started. Then what? Plus, people will talk. I can just hear it now. They'll say I tricked you. What if your parents think I tricked you into this?"

"Well, it's not true, so don't even say it, Faith."

"People *will* talk, you know it's true. They'll say we were stupid and careless and start all kinds of rumors. They'll stare at me . . . at my belly . . . my big fat belly. They'll talk behind our backs. They'll say we were . . . you know . . . they'll say I'm . . ."

"Don't say it, Faith," I said more sternly.

"They'll say I trapped you into marrying me."

"Geez, Faith, you make it sound so . . . I don't know what."

"You know how people are. They'll say this baby is

... illegitimate."

"STOP! Not if we're married! Besides, Mary wasn't married when she gave birth to Jesus."

"Come on, Noah. This is not the same thing. An angel didn't come to me in the middle of the night and no one spoke to you in a dream. We're in deep trouble. We never should've . . . see, this is what we get. We're being punished. I'm being punished."

Faith was understandably getting worked up.

"Faith, relax. Please. We'll get through this. We're not being punished. And, it's not like we're the only ones doing it."

"Doing it? We were *doing it?*" she scolded, letting me know that I had offended her.

My hands went up and grabbed her solid, slender arms.

"No! We were never just *doing it.* I'm sorry I said it like that. Don't ever think of us that way. I love you, Faith. Everything we've done is nothing less than love. And this baby is no punishment. I mean, I *was* trying to prevent this from happening, but it happened anyway. Besides, they say that babies are a blessing, right? We were being so careful. It's the only explanation. Our parents will eventually come around. Don't worry. Please don't worry."

I gathered her trembling body into mine and tenderly kissed the top of her head.

"We're going to have a baby, Faith. You're having *our* baby!" I whispered in her ear.

At the sound of my confident affirmation, I could feel the tension leaving her as she sank farther into my chest.

"We're going to have a baby!" I whispered as the idea of parenthood danced before me and my excitement began to supersede my fear—for about a second, maybe two.

I'm going to be a father . . .

Faith and I spent the remaining hours we had together batting about all of our possible options. I tried to convince her that I was willing to withdraw from Boston

University to stay with her. We would marry, hopefully with our parents' blessings. I would delay school, get a job, and maybe I could get my degree at a later date.

I could only hope that Faith was fully convinced of my commitment to do what was right: what I truly believed I wanted to do . . . needed to do.

No . . . this is definitely what I want to do. Hell, I'm going to be a father! Faith and I are going to have a baby!

Sadly, the baby died a week later. Two weeks' later, my parents shipped me off to Boston University.

I have to tell you, those remaining weeks before I departed for school were so strained. In fact, Faith and I spent more time apart, than together. And, Faith was no longer her sweet self. She stopped writing and wouldn't return my calls. I wrote to her every day. I called her every night, but her mother said Faith wasn't available or wasn't feeling well. When Faith returned to work at the diner, I resorted to dropping by unannounced. She wouldn't even look at me or talk to me. In fact, she made sure someone else waited my table.

In an act of desperation, on my last visit, I waited in my car until after her shift was over. When she exited the front door, untying her apron, I ran up to meet her.

"What are you doing here?" she groused.

"Faith, we need to talk. Please. Why won't you talk to me?"

Ill-timed, her mother pulled into the parking lot. Faith started moving toward her mother's car when I instinctively grabbed her by the arm.

"Let me go!" Faith roared as she yanked her arm from my grasp.

Her mother pulled the car up alongside us.

"Noah!" her mother admonished as she rolled down the driver's side window.

"Please, Mrs. Cuthbertson . . ."

While Faith's mother stared and studied me, Faith stormed around to the passenger side and slipped in without a word. Even "I hate you" or "We're through" would have been better than saying nothing.

Surprisingly, Mrs. Cuthbertson offered the only kind words: "I'm sorry, Noah," which was odd given what she must have just witnessed. Then Mrs. Cuthbertson rolled up her window and drove off with Faith in the passenger seat, looking away.

I had come so far and waited so long to pour out my heart to Faith, but for reasons I couldn't quite fathom, she wanted nothing to do with me.

I could certainly understand her being agitated or depressed. I mean, I was depressed, too. OK, so maybe I couldn't fully grasp what she was going through, but I would have been willing to listen. She wouldn't even give me the chance. If she needed more time, all she needed to do was tell me. I would have willingly delayed school; even move to North East to help her through it, if that's what it would take. I would even suggest that we get married anyway and go forward with our plans, regardless of our loss. (Looking back, I realize, now, that I had no clue what I was even contemplating.)

I don't cry very often. But my heart was breaking for her . . . and for me. When our baby died, we had lost everything. Everything about us had ended with the death of our child. I had never felt so devastated in all my life.

Before she had told me of her pregnancy, we had made plans to go out to dinner the night before I was to leave for Boston. I had made reservations well in advance at one of my parents' favorite restaurants: Schaefer's Canal House, in Chesapeake City.

The afternoon of our previously arranged "date," I took another chance in the hope that Faith would at least keep to our plans. I called to confirm. Her mother answered the phone. Faith again refused to take my call.

"Please, Mrs. Cuthbertson, I understand your being upset with me . . . I am so sorry for what happened."

"She's not taking any calls, Noah."

"Can I at least come down to say goodbye?"

"It's probably best that you don't."

Whenever Faith and I had talked about Boston, she always reminded me that she didn't believe in goodbyes. Except . . . apparently, she did.

I decided to risk it all.

"Mrs. Cuthbertson, please tell Faith that I love her, and I always will. I will wait, if she wants me to."

There was a pause before Mrs. Cuthbertson softly spoke.

"I will tell her. Goodbye, Noah. Good luck at school."

FAITH

Telling my parents was one of the most difficult things I have ever done in my life. No matter how well you think you can predict someone's reaction to bad news, there's no possible way to calculate the response to the "pregnant, unwed, teenage daughter" pronouncement. I know now that when it comes to a child, a parent is defenseless to mask their devastation. When I sat down at the table with my mother and father, and finally got around to my confession, I was already exhausted from the stress of anticipation and the very physical changes that were tiring my body. When the words came out of my mouth, my mother stopped breathing. Her eyes got big and round, and her jaw dropped. I was braced for rage. Later, I realized that what I had actually witnessed was indeed rage . . . and fear . . . and disbelief . . . and a sense of helplessness, all cut together to form a special kind of betrayal, as if I had not paid attention to the one thing she had warned me about since I had gotten my first period. It was as if I had had no appreciation for all that they had done for me since my birth.

My mother gasped, "Oh, my God. Are you sure about this, Faith? Are you absolutely sure?"

"Yes," I numbly answered. "I took a home pregnancy test a few days ago. It was positive. Today, I took a second one, just to be sure. I got the same result. I haven't had my period in two months."

My dad winced when I mentioned my menstrual cycle. How uncomfortable.

"How could you let this happen, Faith? What on earth were you thinking?" Dad asked, clearly mortified.

I didn't know how to answer him. My queasy nervousness languished in nauseating silence. What do you say to your father when he asks a question like that, about a thing like *that*? He raised me. He trusted me. He expected better of me. My father lowered his face into his hands as if he could never look at me again. If I had to guess, he was surrendering to his obvious inability to fix this *thing*, just as he would have if I were talking about a broken toy, a leaky raft, or a dent in the family car. But, there was nothing he could do to repair the damage I had done this time. He was likely coming to grips with the loss of my innocence and his assumed failure as a parent. For my dad, I was no longer his unblemished little girl. There was no undoing what I had done.

In my mother's eyes, I could see her hurt. She was reacting to a future—my future—being flushed down the toilet: swirling downward, irretrievably gone. Truth be known, she, too, never looked at me the same again. For my mom, I had committed a high crime, the penalty was life, and I knew she was right.

At a loss for words, yet unable to bear the silence, I blurted out, "We were being careful. We didn't mean for this to happen. I really don't know how it happened."

(Children in trouble will say the dumbest things.)

"WE ARE NOT STUPID, FAITH!" my mother roared.

Tempers detonated like a catastrophic explosion.

"Mom, I'm telling you, Noah and I were being careful ... and I mean *very* careful."

"Shut up! Shut up! Just stop!" My dad yelled as he jumped up from the table where he had previously expected to eat his dinner in peace.

"Where is he?" my father thundered. "I'm going to pull him apart."

I had never heard my dad speak with such aggressive malice toward another person. It was frightening.

"He's not here, Dad. He's home. It's not his fault," I foolishly pleaded.

"The hell it isn't!" My dad's face reddened and swelled. I thought he might blow up. "Did he force himself on you? Did he? I'll kill the bastard."

"No, Dad. It was an accident."

"An accident? AN ACCIDENT? How dare . . ." And then my father choked on the words and thoughts that were escalating in his head before setting forth his edict.

"He's not to set foot on this property again, young lady. Do you understand me? How dare he? You're so young . . . too young. Jesus!"

My dad's stomach began heaving, causing his body to lurch forward and his throat to close and gag on whatever was trying to come up. Before I knew what was happening, he bolted down the hall for the bathroom where he made it to the bowl in time to begin puking up what little food was in his stomach. He was in the same little room where I had failed my pregnancy tests. The bathroom: our family's personal crisis center.

My mother chased after him. Exasperated. Probably afraid to be left alone to confront me. I remained at the table, isolated by a great divide known as Harsh Reality. On one side, my childhood innocence was drifting farther away as I tried to cope with my parents' reactions; and on the other was the judgment and condemnation we, as a family, were about to face. The news would surely spread like wildfire throughout the small community. My mother was doomed to feel as though all her years of child rearing had been deficient, a waste of her time. Her one job in life was to take care of my father and raise my sister and me. Everything she thought she had accomplished had been vaporized in a searing flash of two words: "I'm pregnant."

I observed it all as she remained outside the bathroom door, hunched over and broken, listening to my dad and his dry heaves. She waited for him to reemerge. She needed him beside her, to help her cope with each stark second that was now redefining our lives. I had greatly underestimated how my news would change their lives, as well.

During the entire ordeal, the brutality of their agonizing disappointment was the most difficult to bear. After my father returned to the table, he never sat down. Standing over me, he hopelessly tried to gain some control over the situation, not immediately realizing that it was totally out of his hands. The remainder of the night was a roller coaster of extreme emotional outbursts. We had moments of exhaustive shouting, interspersed with short interludes of despondent anguish, all concluding with absolutely nothing being resolved. My older sister, Hope, had been shooed away several times. I had no idea how much she had heard. Meanwhile, a little zygote, continued to innocently grow inside me.

After I had gone to bed, I overheard Mom talking to someone on the telephone. It was Mrs. McKenna, Noah's mother. Mrs. McKenna had called to ask if she could pay a visit to our home the following day. My mother reluctantly consented. Other than that, there was not much else to say or do.

That night, in bed, I lay awake, horrified and feeling sick. My body's natural numbing anesthesia was wearing off. I had told my parents. And in the end, I knew I was the one who would remain responsible to carry the burden of what was to come. It was *my* future that was lost. *I* would be the ultimate sacrifice. Lying in the dark and staring at the ceiling, every passing minute was spent in a replay of regretful events.

If only I could take back time.

Mom kept me home from school the next day. Mrs. McKenna came to visit with one mission in mind: to convince my mother—and me—that an abortion would be the best thing for me, and her son. She offered to make the arrangements so that I could be "treated" by the best doctors, and she was willing to pay for the procedure and any other expenses incurred.

Abortion . . .
A way out . . .
I could go on with my life. Noah could go off to school.
Noah . . . did I really want him to go away to school?
What are the chances that maybe this pregnancy was meant to keep us together?

How shallow of me to even think about it that way.

"Thou shalt not murder."

What's one more "Thou Shalt Not?" I'm already on my way to hell. I could at least try to salvage what's left of my life on earth.
Is it the right thing to do? Mrs. McKenna seems to think so. And look at her; she has everything, so she should know.

If I keep the baby, Noah and I could get married. I'd have to give up my job . . . maybe . . . or Mom might be willing to babysit. Noah could find work, I'm sure. He's so smart and likeable.

I could be happy in a little house. I don't need much to survive.

Would Noah be happy? Could he survive it? He comes from so much wealth.

This is definitely not the way I thought life would turn out.

My life could go on if I had an abortion. Life could go on for everyone . . . well, almost everyone.

Is it the right thing to do? I mean, it's really not a baby yet, right? It's just a . . . condition . . . right? It could be "treated."

The sooner, the better, I suppose. That's what Mrs. McKenna said, and Mom, albeit reluctantly, has agreed.

And so, Mrs. McKenna wasted no time and immediately proceeded to have everything taken care of. There was one condition, though: We had to promise to never tell Noah what we had done. As far as he was to be concerned, the baby had died.

"Noah needs to leave for Boston with a clear head and no distractions. If we tell him the baby died, it's not exactly a lie," Mrs. McKenna assured me.

Mom faced me directly and concluded that because "Noah and you (meaning me) are so young, it would be for the best."

My mother drove me to New York City—a location far enough away from both families and our respective communities—where doctors were waiting to interview us. The following day, if my mother and I were still sure about *"my"* decision, they would perform the "procedure." Mrs. McKenna had prearranged everything, as promised. She obviously had a lot of friends and possessed a large amount of clout in good ole NYC.

However, Mrs. McKenna elected to stay home in West Chester, Pennsylvania, far away from the mess I had made.

I was fortunate, I guess. Everything took place in a hospital. I didn't have to go to a clinic and walk through a gauntlet of angry protestors hurling obscenities in my direction. Yet, as I quietly entered the hospital's busy main lobby, I felt as though I was carrying some deep, dark, dirty secret into a sterile environment. Knowing what I was about to do, I couldn't help but feel as if I had just arrived from some skanky alleyway and at any moment my secret would be exposed. Then the "Evangelicals" would come seeping out of the stark, cold concrete walls, point at me with gnarly fingers from years of turning thin crinkly pages of their Bibles, and pronounce me a "Baby Killer."

"Thou shalt not kill."
What if I'm found out?
What if Noah finds out what I'm about to do . . . or what I've done?

Upon entering a small, secluded waiting room, I approached the receptionist's window with my mother right behind me. Answering the questions asked of me became my confessional. I whispered each response, though no one, other than my mother, was near enough to hear.

The receptionist then handed me a clipboard and asked me to complete the information required. Looking around the room for a place to sit, to some relief, I noticed that we were not alone. I was not the "only one." Two young women sat huddled in a corner. One was very nervous; her legs were jittering as she sat bent over her knees. The other woman had a hand laid on her friend's back to lend a supportive touch, hoping to calm her down.

My mother—the same one who never had much to say to me—leaned over and whispered to the trembling woman, "Are you OK, dear?"

The frightened woman looked up. She was older than I was, old enough to be considered a legal adult.

"Everything will be just fine once this is over with," she snarled.

Her consoling friend let out a sigh. "Turns out her boyfriend is already married. Can you believe it? Apparently, having a baby would be a huge inconvenience for him, so she had to make a choice."

"Oh, dear," my mother muttered softly. "And you're sure about this?" she asked the frightened woman.

"I'm sure I can't raise a child on my own!" she snapped back.

My mother slid back into her seat. I tugged on her sleeve.

"Mom, are *we* doing the right thing?"

"We've been over this, Faith. You and Noah are too young. You have your whole lives ahead of you. This is right for *you*," Mom whispered.

I immediately went to work on the questionnaire. My eyes were blurry from the long ride north, and depression seemed to accompany me everywhere I went since the procedural decision had been made. I tried to hide my answers from my mother, keenly aware that she was reading a magazine but looking over my shoulder from time to time, all the time. The questions ranged from "When was your last menstrual cycle?" to "Did your doctor fully explain the procedure?" In between were numerous questions about my method(s) of birth control and basically asking if I understood that I was aborting a "fetus" and terminating my pregnancy.

That's when a nurse entered the waiting room and called my name. I stood and looked back at my mom. I could see the tears welling up in her eyes.

"It'll be fine, Faith. I'll be right here," she eked out. The other two women were staring at me, just daring me to turn around and walk out.

I made my way through the door and followed the nurse. She escorted me down a hallway, telling me her name and offering some semblance of small talk. Her voice became muffled and distant. My vision narrowed under the stress of it all.

I feel like I'm going to pass out.

Just hang in there. In a matter of minutes they'll have me under and it will soon be over, like it never happened.

"Like it never happened," my thoughts echoed.

Dressed in a thin hospital gown, I followed directions and lay down on the cold gurney. My hands slid over my belly as if to say goodbye to my baby, the little peanut growing inside me. Tears. Cloaked sobbing began catching in my throat.

"Faith, everything's going to be OK," I heard the nurse whisper as she gently placed her hand on my shoulder. I had already signed a dozen papers and we were well on our way.

"Oh, dear God, what am I doing?"

Though my mother was nearby, somewhere in the waiting room, I had never felt so alone and so helpless. I wasn't so sure that I was doing the right thing. But, after all, my mother and Noah's mother were older and wiser than I, and they certainly thought this was the direction that I should go.

"Faith, I'm going to place this mask over your mouth and nose. Just relax and breathe deep," the nurse said. That's when I realized I was being strapped down and my feet were being raised into stirrups. So much for my fear of exposing my body "from the waist down."
There was no turning back. I was so young then.

Nothing was ever said to Noah, other than the baby had died. My phone call was brief. I said what I had been coached to say, and then I abruptly hung up. I couldn't bear to hear the immediate anguish in his voice. I couldn't even say, "I love you," because I didn't deserve to hear those words in return, or any consolation, from Noah.

CHAPTER THREE

FAITH

Seeing Noah again was difficult at best. Sixteen years later and he hadn't changed all that much, except for two things: his full head of hair was receding and he had become a pastor. I still remember the day, ten years ago, when my mother found out that Noah was going to be installed at her church.

* * *

"Noah! The very same Noah McKenna that you went steady with is going to be our new pastor," my mother proudly announced in 1984, as if she had forgotten about the little abortion thing, the little lie that we had kept from him. Bizarre.

After receiving the news and after he had made the move to North East, Maryland, I had vowed to stay away from him and my mother's church, to avoid him at all costs. However, when my father passed away in 1985, I could no longer avoid Pastor Noah McKenna. My mother—very oddly—demanded that Pastor Noah officiate the service.

"It's what your father would have wanted, Faith. Believe it or not, he was very fond of Noah," she said straight-faced and with total sincerity.

In what world is that even possible?

"How is that possible? The last time I mentioned Noah's name; Dad was going to rip him apart."

"You've got to believe in miracles, Faith. The first thing Noah did before accepting the position was come to your father and me and asked for our forgiveness. Your father gave him an earful, mind you. I don't think I've ever heard your father swear that much."

"Then what?"

"Noah begged your father, again, for his forgiveness. He broke down crying, saying that he would have loved . . . well, never mind."

"He cried?"

"It's history, Faith. Forget about it."

"You don't just forget about it, Mom. Well, maybe for stretches at a time, but not . . . How could I ever look at Noah and not think about it? How can *you* look at Noah and not think about it?"

"I don't know, Faith. I don't know. He's a better man now."

I thought it best to let her remark slide because what she had failed to realize was that Noah had always been a good man.

"So, then what happened?"

"Then your father hugged him."

"What?"

"Your father knows what happened, Faith."

"Did Daddy tell Noah . . . about the abor . . .?"

"No, no. He knew it would kill Noah. However, he did ask Noah not to speak a word of your 'tragic pregnancy' to anyone."

"And Noah gave him his word?"

"Yes."

"Of course, he did. Then what?"

"Your father told Noah not to expect him in church."

"Huh. And still, you believe Dad would want a memorial service and for Noah to conduct it?"

"Yes."

"You don't feel the least bit awkward about this? About Noah?"

"No. Should I?"

"Mom, we lied to him!"

"Faith, you didn't lie, not technically. And you need to let it go. Noah is better off not knowing. Otherwise, he'd be carrying it around everyday and maybe, just maybe, he wouldn't have gone to school, or into the ministry. He's an excellent pastor."

"How is any of this remotely possible? Don't you feel some remorse? Some guilt?"

"Faith, please, let it go. Everything has worked out for the best. Look at you! You and Tyler are starting a family of your own now."

"Yes, we are," I responded quietly as I patted my little baby bump and stretched my aching back.

Indeed, after Noah had arrived in North East to pastor my mother's church, he and my dad had somehow miraculously reconciled. One year later, Noah would perform a beautiful memorial service honoring my dad's life.

At my father's service, I sat in the front row with my mother on one side of me, and my husband on the other. I was a little uncomfortable with the circumstances. But, quite honestly, no one there knew the *real* truth except my mother and I, and she seemed quite at ease with it. She smiled at Noah each time he said something that pleased her, wiped away a few tears, and then bowed her head in prayer after the last hymn.

I, on the other hand, was a watershed of tears. I reflected back on how my dad had taught me how to swim, how to sail, and how to fish. But he didn't stop there. My dad felt I needed to know how to change the oil in my car, and how to change a tire, to name a few of the life skills he had passed on to me. He wanted me to be self-sufficient and independent. I think he saw me as an extension of himself, unlike my girlish older sister who was only interested in nail polish and accessories. But most of all, I remembered how hard he had worked to provide for our family. No matter how dogged-tired he was my dad always had kind and loving words for my mom, my sister, and me.

Sometimes, I still catch myself dwelling on how upset my dad was that night sixteen years ago. How I regretted the pain I had inflicted and how he had privately carried the burden with him all the way to his death. I would miss him dearly. I would always miss the security of knowing that he was there for me, even in his silent agony.

During the memorial service, I tried not to stare at Noah for fear of being caught. It was true: I had loved Noah like no other. But in the end, my history would include the wounding of my father, the betrayal of Noah, and a baby I decided not to carry to term.

During his message, Noah's words were gentle and full of hope. He was animated and cracked a few jokes at my father's expense. I think my dad would have liked that. Noah even mentioned Abe Cuthbertson's daughter, Faith, whom he had had "the pleasure of knowing for a number of years." My heart melted and my soul, full of guilt, slinked back into the pew. My husband, Tyler, held my hand and lightly massaged my knuckles with his thumb, offering what comfort he could. And then I cried silently into my saturated tissues as I listened to others share their favorite memories of Abe Cuthbertson. Tyler gently put his arms around my shoulders and held me.

Following Noah's closing prayer, the funeral party packed into their cars and my family was escorted to our limo. We were whisked back to my parents' small house on the eastern shore of the North East River. Thankfully, it was a warm, sunny day in May and the luncheon was held outside. Good thing. No way would my parents' small ranch house have been able to accommodate the large number of people who had shown up. I was grateful the ancient septic system survived the afternoon's ordeal. Church members, local waterman, construction workers, plumbers, electricians, carpenters, even several boat owners from local marinas showed up to pay tribute to my dad and "celebrate" his life.

The women's group from Noah's church put out a spread like I had never seen before: corn on the cob; buckets of coleslaw; bowls of potato salad; finger sandwiches of cream cheese and olives, watercress and salmon, tuna salad with sweet pickles, ham and mustard. A group of men drove up in a truck with bushels of fat steamed crabs and a keg of beer. My dad would have loved it.

Why had we not thrown a party like this while he was still alive?

After most of the guests had left, a petite young lady quietly approached me and held out her hand.

"Hello, Faith. My name is Chrissy Webber, a friend of Pastor Noah's. I'm so sorry for your loss."

That was the first time I had met her, and I knew instantly that her status as "a friend of Pastor Noah's," wasn't completely accurate. I could only imagine that she was everything Noah wanted and needed. And, I have to admit that my heart fell to my feet. Noah *was* doing well and would soon be on his way to "happily ever after." It was inevitable . . . *all at my great expense.*

* * *

~ May 1994 ~
Back To The Present

After church on Sunday, I drove my mother home and made lunch for the two of us. With the rising of the noonday sun, the temperature inside and outside the house was rapidly heating up. So we decided to eat out on the landing of the dock where it would be cooler sitting above the chilled water. First I walked Mom down the hill and out onto the gray splintered planks of weathered wooden decking that were nailed down to many doubtful beams and pilings that led out into the deeper water of the North East River. At the end of the dock was a fair-sized landing that barely supported a picnic table, four chairs, and a dilapidated boathouse where we had stored life jackets, oars, and inner tubes. On the landing, one could sit and spend the day listening to the water lap up against the slow sloping shoreline, while boats hummed up and down the river.

After Mom had settled into her chair, I ran back up to the house to retrieve our lunch. Her large serving tray was propped up on the kitchen counter in the very same spot it had been stored years ago when I lived there during my childhood. Mom had carried plates of food and pitchers of iced tea down to the dock using that very tray. I pulled it out and I placed our lunch and glasses of ice water onto it, balancing the weight just as Mom had taught me. Lifting the tray was like taking a trip down memory lane, except now I was the "mom." Indeed, I was missing my own two little girls back in Seattle with their dad. I would call them later in the day, remembering they were on Pacific Time.

"Nothing compares to the Seattle coastline," my husband had boasted years ago when he first announced that we were moving across the country. "Wait and see, Faith. You're going to love it out there!" Nine years ago, "the dirt still fresh on my father's grave" and I was about to give birth, I wasn't so easily convinced.

Now, sitting on the dock that overlooked the North East River, I knew that Tyler was right about the area surrounding Seattle. It *is* absolutely breathtaking. However, there is something innately comfortable about being back home, on my own water. Water that I knew like the back of my hand. Water that ran slowly past the weathered dock and left its tidal markings on the crooked pilings. Water that gently kissed the shoreline with a quiet lisp. Water that smelled of seaweed and mud at low tide, and glimmered a blue-gray in the bright overhead sun of summer. The water where we had scattered my father's ashes into the outgoing tide. Water that seemed to understand me. This would always be my home. This was where I felt safe, where my heart rate slowed and my blood pressure dropped. Everything in my life still aligned itself on the North East River of the Chesapeake Bay.

Mom ate half of her sandwich and barely lowered the level of ice water in her glass before lighting up a cigarette.

"Mom! I thought you quit!"

"What's the use? I'm going to die sooner or later anyway. We're all going to die one day, you know."

"Mom, I really wish you wouldn't say those things or do that around me."

Laying her head back and closing her eyes, my mother took another draw. Within minutes, she was softly snoring. I reached over and gently slid the cigarette through her fingers and tossed it into the water. With a sizzling spit, it was extinguished and began drifting away with the current.

I probably shouldn't have done that. Littering . . . it's disgusting.

Mom's return to her smoking habit was something that my sister had not mentioned. My older sister, Hope, lived nearby. Since Mom's accident, Hope usually checked in on our mother twice a day. However, Hope's husband needed to take an extended business trip to London and she had the opportunity to go along. So, she had asked me to come back East to housesit. I convinced myself that it would be good to spend some quality time with Mom, though dealing with her reinstated bad habit was not something I had counted on.

I looked back over the dock to see if I could retrieve the doused cigarette butt. Unfortunately, it had drifted too far. The tide and the breeze were running in the same direction, speeding the used carbon filter away from me. Watching the disappearing cigarette butt float up-river as if it were a small blade of grass, I accepted my littering indictment and sat my own butt down on the edge of the dock to contemplate my guilt.

Swinging my feet over the edge and dangling them just above the water, I soon felt like a child again. Because it was coming on high tide, my feet easily reached the surface of the water, especially if I slid my buns out to the very edge. I kicked and splashed just like I used to when I was little, except now I was no longer required to wear a life jacket whenever I was on the dock or in a boat.

Reclined in her chair, Mom continued to quietly snore.

I scanned the opposite shoreline, almost a mile across the water, and sighed heavily. Life had been good on the North East River. It was a good place to grow up. Though we weren't wealthy, we were rich in every other way. As I recalled my blessings, I looked back at the house to conjure up some of my favorite memories. That's when a beam of light caught my eye and distracted me. It was coming from within the boathouse. At first, I thought it might be the sun reflecting off the thin glass windowpane by the rickety door. I squinted and put my hand up to my forehead, creating a visor, with hopes of getting a better look at what was causing the brilliant luminescence.

No . . . I don't think it's a reflection. It appears to be coming from inside.

Mom coughed, waking herself.
"I'm ready to go back now," she overtly hinted.
I looked back at the boathouse. All had gone dark.

Moving Mom up the small incline in baby steps took a lifetime. Her mobility had definitely been affected by her injury. Her breathing quickened and labored, probably more as a result of her smoking relapse.
"Mom, you need to stop smoking. That stuff is going to kill you."
"Oh, hush," she panted.
Once we reached the concrete walkway that circled the house, Mom stopped to catch her breath.
"Mom, do you keep a light on in the boathouse? Is it on a timer or something?"
"No," she huffed.
"In the boathouse, there was a light that was on—for how long, I don't know—and then it shut itself off before we started back to the house."
"No one's been in that boathouse for years, Faith," she said, sounding rather annoyed.

"Maybe it *was* a reflection, but I'm pretty sure it came from inside."

"Reflections can create some strange illusions, especially on the water," she commented further.

She coughed and hacked as if speaking a full sentence was too much.

That night, after my mother had gone to bed, I sat in the family room with a book and a glass of red wine. The room was dark, lit only by a single floor lamp positioned by my end of the sofa. It would still be daylight on the West Coast. It was time to call my husband and the girls.

Tyler answered immediately as if he had been sitting by the phone waiting.

"Hello, Darling! How was your day? How's your mom?"

"Tyler," I cooed, "It's so good to hear your voice. Are the girls nearby?"

"Yes, they are." Tyler turned his head away from the phone and called out to Charlie and Maddie, "Girls! Your mother's on the phone!"

"Charlie" is a term of endearment for Charlotte that evolved during her first year. "Maddie" was Madison's intended nickname.

I could hear the girls giggling and their chaotic footsteps in the background as they ran toward their father. I could envision them laughing and jumping up on the sofa, cozying up next to Tyler so they could hear my voice. Tyler said they were in their PJs and about ready for bed. For sure, Charlie was probably wearing her glasses, propped somewhat crookedly on the bridge of her little nose. Maddie would be holding on to her favorite stuffed rabbit.

"Mommy, Mommy! Where are you?"

"I'm in Maryland, at Grandmom's house. Remember?"

"Oh …" Maddie quietly recalled.

"We're several hours ahead of you, so it gets dark here earlier."

"Well, that's no fun," Charlie remarked, though I doubted that she fully understood the whole concept of time zones.

"When are you coming home, Mommy?" Maddie whimpered, completely opening my heart at its weakest seam.

"In a couple of weeks, so be good for Daddy. OK?"

"Of course!" Charlie chirped.

The girls sat and listened as best they could while I spoke of Mom's health, and when they got bored, they scooted off the sofa and on to other things more entertaining before bedtime on the West Coast.

"And how are *you* doing?" Tyler asked, assuming that being a caretaker for my mother had worn me out in just twenty-four hours.

"Quite well, actually. Mom has slowed down considerably, though. But all in all, I guess she's doing OK."

"That's good to hear."

"However, she has taken up smoking again. Ugh."

"That's too bad."

"Right? And I think she smokes inside the house too. It's disgusting."

"I'm sorry to hear that. But, I'm sure it's hard for her—being alone and all. There could be worse things, I suppose."

"Really? I can't think of one."

"How's life on the river?"

"Well, I must admit, I've missed it. Being here takes me back. Familiar sights and sounds . . . it hasn't changed all that much. Same old dock . . . same water . . . different boats going up and down the river, now . . . except . . ."

"Except what?"

I stopped. I realized Tyler would think me silly to obsess over a light inside the boathouse. He would pooh-pooh it just like my mom, thinking I was overreacting to the reflection of the sun or some other simple phenomenon. And truthfully, I knew I always obsessed about things that were left unresolved. It was my nature. And God bless Tyler, he had learned to grin and bear it. For me, when something struck me, I was always convinced that more investigation was necessary. But this was different. There was something personal about that light.

"Oh, nothing. Just some unremarkable shells I'd found in the sand."

"Forever collecting shells," Tyler murmured.

"Yeah," I whispered. "I wish you and the girls were here."

"You just got there! Homesick already?"

"No. Not really. I just miss everyone."

"It'll fly by quickly. You'll see. You'll be back home, in Seattle, before you know it."

The following morning, after Mom had had her breakfast and was seated in her favorite chair to watch "Judge Judy," I grabbed the boathouse keys from the hook beside the back door and made my escape down to the dock. The air was heating up quickly again, and a fine haze hovered just above the surface of the water. Everything was still and damp, covered in morning dew. Walking across the creaky boards, I was almost giddy with youthful, adventurous adrenaline. I felt like I was fourteen again, seeking out another unsolved mystery in my young life, some phenomenon that no one else had discovered. Reaching the side of the boathouse that faced the river, I turned and addressed the old door, grabbing hold of the ancient rusted padlock. After twisting and turning the key in the corroded lock cylinder, I pulled down hard on the mechanism several times. With some added manhandling, it stubbornly popped loose. The door wobbled and teetered unsteadily, scraping along the dock as I tried to pull it open. The door hinges were in worse shape than the lock. Once the door gave way, I was immediately struck by the musty smell that invaded my nostrils and plastered my face as I entered the ramshackle boathouse.

Ugh, when was the last time this place was aired out?

Upon my first step inward, everything went to black and white. A flurry of dust particles flew about the interior caused by the sudden vacuum of the door, sucking up the thick coating of powdered mildew and mold that covered every surface.

I waved my arms trying to clear the heavy air so I could see past my nose. It only made the situation worse and it didn't take long for the mixture of floating molecules of mold to complete their assault on my sinuses and advance down my throat. I coughed with a mighty hack, actually tasting the miniscule spores as they came back up and clung to the roof of my mouth. It tasted worse than fuzzy, spoiled grapes.

"Jesus Almighty!" I shouted. "This air is toxic enough to kill someone!"

I backed out of the boathouse and spit out what insidious residue I could into the water. Standing up straight again, I turned and watched as the dense dust inside the boathouse danced in the light that was peeking through pinholes in the roof and eaves, as well as the floorboards. I knew the light originated from a single source, but to be entering from so many different angles? It made the scene unearthly, more like something from a sci-fi movie.

While waiting for the biohazard to settle, I walked farther out onto the edge of the dock to breathe in some clean air and contemplate several theories that were swimming around in my head. There was a quiet hum as a lone boat made its way down the channel. Small waves lapping the shoreline would soon be amplified by the late arrival of the boat's wake, pushing modest tufts of landed seaweed back and forth.

"Mom! There you are!" I heard plain as day.

"What?"

"I thought I'd find you here."

I looked around. No one was in sight.

I looked up the hill toward the house. Everything was quiet with the exception of a few leaves that rustled in the trees situated between here and there. A light breeze had passed through. Then, all was calm again.

The boathouse . . . I had left the door open. I cautiously returned to the entrance. I stood and listened. Nothing. I peered in. The heavier dust had settled, leaving a hazy veil to linger. No one was inside. But "something" *was* there. A memory? Many memories. This was where Noah and I had sequestered ourselves when his family was down on their yacht and we were in search of much desired privacy.

* * *

In another life, Noah and I would sneak down to the dock and into the boathouse. Inside, we would take the lounge cushions and lay them on the floor, and that's where we would stay together, talking and playing quietly. Lying side by side, Noah's hand would leisurely find its way beneath my T-shirt, exploring and sending electrified spasms into the region behind the zipper of my jean shorts. Soon, my shirt was off and so was his. Skin against skin, he would finally reach around and release the clasps of my bra. Noah's lips would work their way down my neck and across my shoulders until they had found the places that would drive me crazy. Taking me into his mouth and teasing me with his tongue, my head would dizzily arch back as I prayed he would never stop. Pulling a beach blanket over us, we would eventually find ourselves naked and breathless. But Noah was careful, or so we had thought.

How I had wanted those hours of passionate and torturous play to never end.

* * *

I leaned back against the doorframe, swooning at the very thought of him. My senses remembered the smell of him, the feel of him just on the edge.

I stepped farther into the boathouse and stood in the middle of its cramped quarters, about the same place where Noah and I would lie together on the floor. That's when I noticed a single beam of light reaching through a gap in the floorboards. It was intense and direct, much like when the sun sharply penetrates through a hole in dense cloud cover.

It must be coming from the sun's rays reflecting off the water below the dock. Perhaps the angle of the sun and the extreme low tide are combining to create this effect?

I was drawn to the mysterious streak of light. It beckoned me to kneel down on the floor and soak in those summer memories and lusty feelings once again. However, the conditions were not exactly the same, not by a long shot. The floor was filthy, likewise everything within the four walls of the small shed. And I was no longer naïve and innocent about the ways of men, or my own desires, for that matter. I was married and had children of my own now. Back in Seattle, I was living a safe and comfortable life. I had somehow managed to escape what I thought was my ill-fated destiny sixteen years ago.

The boathouse was daring me to venture back to that dangerous time when everything was new and exhilarating. Those were such lusty days. I would live from weekend to weekend, waiting for the McKenna family to return to their yacht at Bay Boat Works so I could be with Noah. I loved being loved—hearing it in his words, the sensations of his touch, and the heat of his arousal. It was all so new and thrilling. I couldn't get enough of him then. Aching and urging him on to complete my fulfillment. I wanted all of him. But Noah was the one with all of the fortitude and restraint.

I took one final look around before walking out.

Closing the door, I let the lock hang unengaged, dangling on its clasp. Sighing, I exhaled and said a silent goodbye to my past.

Returning to the fresh air while standing on the dock above the river, I took a deep breath.

Those days are gone . . .

Remaining still, like a statue with living ears, I listened once again. Only the ripples of the river below could be heard.

All right. Enough is enough. Everything happened so long ago . . . I'm just tired and a little overwhelmed, that's all.

I straightened the chairs around the table, and then walked past the boathouse window now coated with the fine dust that had been stirred up inside. The light from within was receding, probably because the rising tide was narrowing the angle of the sun, I theorized. In my heart of hearts, I knew that eventually I would need to solve the mystery, but not right then. I had already gone too far down memory lane for one day. It didn't feel safe to linger there any longer. The light was probably something simple anyway.

As I made my way back up to the house, the nagging sensation of something left undone began to gnaw at me from the inside out.

NOAH

~ Recollections of the Past ~

In 1984, about ten years ago, I had been called to a small church in North East, Maryland, just off Rt. 272, about seven miles north of the Turkey Point Lighthouse. Chrissy had moved to North East from Belair, Maryland, just one year earlier, after receiving a professorship at the Cecil County Community College. As destiny would have it, she eventually came to "check out" our little church several weeks after my installation.

Ashamedly, I never told her that I had applied to and accepted the call of that particular church with the hope of reestablishing a prior relationship. You see, I had never given up on Faith. At that age, as a hopeless romantic, I was not ready to let go of Faith and all that I believed awaited us.

Still, Chrissy and I became fast friends. She was full of life and strong in her faith, yet she never took herself too seriously. Also, she was a good influence on me. Spending enormous amounts of time with her was instrumental in helping me to loosen up and not to be so stiff and consumed with the way "a man of the cloth" should be perceived by others.

"They have to know you're human too," Chrissy used to say. "How is anyone to believe that you can actually sympathize with their struggles if you're always projecting some 'holier than thou' image?"

Despite how much I enjoyed being around Chrissy, I guarded my heart and kept her at arm's length for many months until someone blatantly suggested that I should "take her out." Chrissy was standing right there, mind you, when this mutual friend of ours had blurted it out. That weekend, on a Saturday night, I took Chrissy out to dinner and a movie.

While dating the vivacious Chrissy Webber, I began ordering a glass of wine with dinner, or a beer at lunch. I began adding edgier jokes to my sermons. I shared some of my lesser youthful crimes with the congregation. I admitted to some of my issues, or my unorthodox responses to things that annoyed me or drove me crazy, like out-of-state drivers who believed their vacation rent, slip fees, or yacht club memberships paid for the right to be lawless on the road and rude to store clerks and the wait staff around town.

With time and a developing casual comfort with each other, Chrissy and I began holding hands in public, or sharing a kiss. We started spending every day together. We were a couple and finally, one night, I told her that I loved her.

I am not proud of how we carried on in her third floor attic apartment after my profession of love. Obviously, we had been two lonely mortals in search of fulfillment.

Yes, I am a pastor. But I am also a carnal man, full of passionate urges and an eventual limit to my ability to hold back, as any other man would have been. I, too, crave the touch of human flesh. As such, I had succumbed to the very type of sin that I had preached against. I had put the pleasure of my flesh before all else. In the heat of the moment, Chrissy assured me that we would be safe. She was on the pill and no one would ever have to know.

It's not like I'm a virgin, I mentally rationalized, as Chrissy and I lay naked and wrapped around each other, hands moving as our lips parted and tongues tangled. Having "been there before" made my capacity to resist all the more impossible.

I stayed the night.

Very early the next morning, I apologized profusely and Chrissy cried.

"I don't regret what happened, Noah," she asserted. "I have been hoping that one day our friendship would become more. Please, please don't let this spoil our chances."

"Chrissy, I don't know what to say. I'm a pastor. This is certainly not the example I should be setting for my congregation. I must abide by my own words, *His* words," I countered, thinking heavenward. Though, I felt like heaven was now ashamed of me, too.

"I love you, Noah. I have from the first day I met you," Chrissy confessed softly. She slowly looked up and into my eyes. "Last night meant everything to me," she mewled.

So sensually drawn to her words, I immediately sat back down on the mattress, beside her, and took her hands into mine and brushed her hair away from her face.

"I love you, Chrissy. But surely you can understand how conflicting this is for me. I just became the biggest hypocrite that ever lived. God clearly warns His teachers not to take His sheep down the wrong path. Look at what I've done."

"No, Noah. You're not guilty of anything other than being human, like the rest of us. You're not a god. You're just Noah McKenna. You're a good man and I love you so much."

"I love you, too. But I'm sure God is not happy with me right now."

"Now, YOU'RE being a hypocrite!" Chrissy said with convicting emphasis. "You're always preaching that God loves us 'no matter what.' Well, if what you've preached is true . . ."

"Don't make light of my responsibilities, Chrissy." I said tersely in response to her glib rationale.

"Listen, Noah. In your own teachings, you've said that God called David 'a man after His own heart' and look at the mess David made. He had an affair and murdered his mistress's husband. And yet, God never stopped loving him. God adored David. That's what you've taught."

"Chrissy, I'm held to a higher standard, so don't go throwing my words back at me."

"They're not *your* words. That story doesn't belong to you. And it shows that not even the best of us is perfect, and that God can still love us, right here, right now."

"And what about how it makes *me* feel? It's so easy for you to excuse everything. You're not the one standing in front of two hundred people every Sunday espousing the doctrines of the church."

"No, I'm not. But perhaps the church shouldn't be so demanding of its servants. Why do you pastors all believe that you have to be little gods running around as perfect, infallible little puppets?"

"Chrissy, don't say that. I've already explained that we are held to a higher standard."

"I *will* say it! And don't misunderstand me. I'm not saying that God asked you to *be* a puppet. You have tied your own church strings onto little martyr sticks, thinking that self-demanded bondage will earn you your way into heaven."

I was offended and turned to leave.

"Wait!" Chrissy shouted. "God doesn't need you to be perfect. He needs you to be human. He needs you to be you, imperfections and all."

In some ordinary way, it sounded so simple. Her words merely mirrored things I had said myself from the pulpit. But I knew—at least for me—it was more complicated than that.

Chrissy persisted. "No one needs to know what happened here last night."

"God knows," I reminded her, ashamedly.

She paused and her tone changed. "Just know that I don't have any regrets. The only thing that I regret is that you will look upon last night as a huge mistake and a cross to be carried upon *your* shoulder, and that you will turn away from me. I love you, Noah McKenna. Can't you be happy about that and what we could have together?"

I turned and grabbed my jacket from a chair near her bedroom door and started to walk out.

Wait, this is not right . . .

I stepped back into her bedroom. Chrissy was still sitting up against the headboard with the covers pulled up around her.

"I think . . . maybe . . . it's just that my head is spinning right now." I reached out and gently lingered a touch upon her cheek and kissed the top of her head.

Quietly, as stealthily as I could, I made my way down the metal fire escape that provided access to her apartment. My car was parked several blocks away.

Driving home to the small parsonage built beside the chapel, I fought with my conscience. I fought with God, asking Him why His strength from within me wasn't strong enough to fight off what I had so desperately desired just hours earlier. I begged Him for His forgiveness. Yet everything—every thought of contrite remorse—was overshadowed by my recollections of a night spent with Chrissy. In the end, like someone on a diet trying not to think of food, I was struggling to conjure up ways to stop thinking of her: naked, beautiful, in the flesh, warm, funny, carefree. The truth was, in effect, that I was using any excuse—as well as my prayers—to dwell upon her and what had happened. She floated in and out of my meditations as I begged God for His forgiveness. One moment praying to God, speaking directly to Him; the next moment recalling the exploration of Chrissy's body and the feel of her hot . . . wet . . . soft skin and how our bodies had come together. I had spent the night with her. I had been enthralled by her and everything that had happened. I knew there would be no turning back, no matter how hard I tried to fight it.

FAITH

~ May 1994 ~
Present Day

During lunch, my mother swore that she had never seen a mysterious light in the boathouse. My fixation on the phenomenon was only succeeding to further solidify my mother's adamant denial. I, in turn, was becoming more and more obsessed with the strange illumination.

"Well, I intend to solve the mystery," I declared resolutely. "I have a hypothesis."

"Fine," my mother replied, as she set down her iced tea. "Do what you have to do. If nothing else, it will keep you occupied."

Once the dishes were rinsed off and in the dishwasher, I made my way back down to the dock.

"Don't fall in!" my mother yelled from the family room as I went out the door.

She will always treat me like a child . . .

As I walked down the slope toward the dock, it was immediately obvious that the tide was running fast and would be extremely low, reaching dead low around five o'clock.

Dead low tide has a very distinct smell, one you never forget, one that lets you know you're home on the banks of the North East River. It's not a bad smell. It's just a very distinct smell . . . heavy . . . you can almost taste it between the hard and soft palate at the top of your mouth. Seaweed infused, damp, and muddy air.

The coming full moon combined with a steady breeze had respectively pulled and pushed the water out of the river, leaving the underpinnings of the dock bare and exposed. The skies were clear and the sun was high above my head. Charlestown was clearly visible on the opposing shore. Like the day before, the weather was going to reach a toasty eighty-seven degrees before it was over. Gulls flew past the boathouse, Carolina wrens and red bellied woodpeckers were singing and chortling in the trees along the shoreline. The day was off to a good start.

How I love the sound of flip-flops on a wooden dock mixed with the hush of small rhythmic swells moving on and off the unusually widened strip of sand just behind me. Once over the water, the air turned crisp and a little cooler. Rounding the boathouse, I peered inside, and sure enough, the interior was illuminated.

"Mom! How do I look?" I distinctly heard coming from inside.

I *knew* that voice. My heart leapt at its sound. The way it said *"Mom"* stirred my inner being, the depths of my soul. The voice was like honey to a raw throat and possessed the comfort of sleeping in your own bed after a long journey.

"So . . . how do I look?" it asked again.

I squinted sharply, my heart racing and the pupils of my eyes dilating as I tried to focus into the unkempt space.
"Where are you?" I asked, the words escaping my mouth without forethought, or realizing how silly it was that I was responding.
"Come on!" someone laughed, coaxing me in.

I pulled open the unlocked door and stepped in, accidently kicking a small object across the floorboards. Dust particles levitated and danced in the light. I stooped to pick up the variegated calcium-colored object to which I had just given the boot. It was a shell, one that I recognized immediately. I turned it over in my hands. Yes, it was definitely the same one. It had the same small chip along its edge from when I had dropped it years ago. I had not seen it in more than a decade and a half. But there it was, in the boathouse, and I was holding it once again, turning it over and over to examine it in my disbelief.

* * *

~ Remembering the events of 1977,
one year after I had met Noah ~

"I brought you a present," Noah said teasingly as he stretched out his arms toward me with his hands close-fisted, "But you have to guess which hand it's in."

Noah had just returned from a trip with his family to Sanibel, Florida. Upon landing in Philadelphia and then chauffeured home to West Chester, he immediately added another hour to his travels by driving south to North East to see me.

Noah always liked to play games. Full of anticipation, he stood before me and waited eagerly for me to play along. My first guess was wrong, of course. Noah laughed out loud and thrust his hands behind his back, pretending to be swapping an item back and forth between them.

"Now guess!" he challenged as he thrust his hands out toward me again.

I touched the other hand.

"No, No!" he laughed even harder. "You're so predictable. Try again."

Noah threw his arms around his back and moved his hands and body erratically.

"All right, this is your last chance," he warned, holding his fists out one more time.

Thinking that I, too, could be a smartass, I touched both of his hands. They flew open and both were empty. Laughing again, Noah grabbed me around my waist, tickling me, which he knew I hated.

"Stop! Stop!" I yelled.

Despite my futile attempts to get away from his twitching fingers, Noah managed to pull me in for a long and fulfilling kiss.

"I missed you, Faith Cuthbertson. I wish you could've come along with us."

At the first touch of his lips, I had stopped struggling. Noah gave me another quick peck before releasing me and reaching into the pocket of his leather bomber jacket. Taking my hands, he placed an object into them. I looked down into my cupped palms.

"It's beautiful! I've never seen one like it!"

"I know, right? I found it on a beach in Sanibel and I brought it back for you."

"Thank you, Noah. Do you know what kind of shell it is?"

"Of course, I do. I looked it up." Typical Noah. He was always in search of answers. "It's a sundial. It's said to have healing powers."

"Healing powers, you say?" I gave him a doubtful look.

"Yes, and its vibrations are soothing to the soul."

"Vibrations, you say. Are you suggesting that I am in need of such prescriptions?" I snarked.

"No, quite the opposite. This shell reminded me of you because when I'm around you . . . you make everything right. You're my sundial."

Noah let that sit for a moment before continuing. He placed his hands under and around mine, still cradling the restorative shell.

"Plus, look at it! It's said to emit compassion, and peace."

"That's a lot for one little shell, Noah."

"Yes, it's *so* you. So full of life . . . and love . . . and passion . . . and what you do to me," he said slowly and deliberately, separating each word or phrase with an urgent kiss.

I inhaled deeply, dizzied by his acclamations . . . and then his aching eagerness.

* * *

~ 1994 ~
Present Day

The sundial shell is lenticular in shape. The top view of the shell displays an intricate white and brown dotted band that spirals and grows wider as it fans out from its apical center. Between each full spiral of the dotted band are solid bands: one of textured caramel, the other a haunting gray-blue. The three contrasting bands accentuate the shell's perfect Fibonacci pattern. Conversely, the sundial's underside is concave. The under and inward spiral, sharply defined by the same distinct patterns, dimensions, and depth, is like peering into an illustrative Egyptian staircase that drifts away with no end, thus earning its nickname "the staircase shell." And then, if turned sideways, one realizes that the shell is made up of one long, hollow calcium carbonate tube that has funneled outward as its resident marine snail had expanded in size over time.

I held the shell to the light and stared into the concave underside. The translucent shell lit up, illuminating the layers and depth of its delicately spiraled staircase. I imagined what it would be like to run around and around, diminishing in size as I traveled its never-ending coil. I felt a tingling lurch in my stomach, and an adrenaline rush swept through my gut as I tried to catch my breath. I had lost the ability to inhale and could feel the immediate onset of suffocation. To my shock and horror, the shell was sucking the wind right out of me. I was being denied oxygen as my lungs painfully constricted. They were going to implode. The weathered walls of the boathouse began to close in on me, yet nothing moved. My vision was folding in on itself as I passed through shrinking layers. I was speeding along an endless coil. Light speed. No air. I was becoming extremely nauseous, likened to sudden seasickness. Sensationally, my body was leaving me. My vision became pixelated, as if blacking out. I couldn't get my bearings—moving, yet unmistakably still. Darkness came creeping through the opened boathouse door, moving like a sheer, black veil. And then, it swallowed me.

How long it lasted, I have no idea. As oxygen re-entered my lungs with intensity and immense speed, I gagged and coughed and had to brace myself against the shelf next to me. The shell remained in my hand. I was coming out of its grip, as though pushed through a birth canal. Air, raw and dry. Light, blinding light. My sight correcting, my respiration steadying, I could feel my organs returning to their life sustaining functions, oxygenated blood coursing through my veins once again.

I remained standing in the boathouse; yet, unless my eyes were deceiving me, the interior of the boathouse had been oddly transformed. The dust had not only settled, it had been evacuated altogether. The roof and the floor no longer allowed sunlight to seep through tiny crevices. Several new, colorful lounge cushions were stacked on the shelves in front of me and new kayak paddles were standing in the corner.

Everything was different except for the sundial that Noah had given me back in 1977 . . . when we were young and in love . . . my first love. Before I had thrown everything away.

"Don't be long, Momma! Darla will be here soon. Then we've gotta go."

Startled again by the voice, I looked around and out past the doorframe. A beautiful young lady was running back up the gentle slope toward the house. Her long strawberry blonde tresses were bouncing in stride with her smooth energetic gait despite the uneven ground under her feet—ground with which I was very familiar.

Instantly, without question or wonder, I knew she was my daughter, my firstborn-to-be. Sixteen years old and full of spunk. I quickly moved outside and turned back to take a second look at the boathouse to make sure it was really there.

The door and its hinges had been replaced. The roof had been repaired and the exterior had received a new coat of stain. The light inside had disappeared. And, I was definitely on the same property, on the same river.

As I studied my surroundings, I was filled with the knowledge of things I had never known before. And as the incoming tide ran swiftly by, history came to me. Each leaf and blade of grass that passed below the dock had a story full of memories: my memories. Things I would have known if I had explored a different tributary in the river of life sixteen years earlier.

Miraculously, my one longing—my one unanswered obsession, my greatest *"what if"*—was there, running up toward the house ahead of me.

What if I had kept the baby?

Still shaky on my feet and navigating with a foggy head, I made my way up the slope. My feet remembered the uneven ground dotted with tree roots and patches of moss. My muscles recalled the zigs and the zags. On the steeper stretches, stairs had been fashioned with the use of carefully spaced railroad ties.

Inside the house, I found Janie in what used to be my old bedroom. She was primping in front of a full-length mirror on the far wall—walls that had been repainted a seafoam green.

"You look beautiful, darling," I whispered. Everything felt so natural, as though I had never missed a day of her life or a beat of her heart.

Janie . . . my daughter . . . my firstborn and the love of my life was standing in front of me. She was tall like her father, and thin and lithe like me in my younger years. Her eyes were blue and bright. Her smile—a smile that never faded or faltered—was like the sun. Being in her presence sent a thrill to my very core. Janie . . . she was here. I was with her! My arms ached to hold her and tell her how much I loved and missed her, yet in some strange way, I had not missed a moment or a memory. I had experienced and retained all of it. I wanted to tell her I was sorry . . . yet there was no reason to be sorry, not "*here*."

My heart was overwhelmed with the sheer joy of watching her. Being *with* her, as any mother is with her child, her firstborn. I enjoyed watching her primp in the mirror, seeing every angle of her life, her physique, her simplicity, the very things her father loved most about her . . . and me.

Janie had a dog, a springer spaniel named Jed, which followed her everywhere. When she was home, he stayed so close to her it was a wonder she never tripped over him. Janie and Jed were like dance partners, carefully anticipating each other's moves, never making a misstep.

Jed. . . . She had named her dog "Jed." "Just because," she had said, "I like the way Janie and Jed sounds!"

Oh, my gosh, she is just like me in so many ways!

Janie had such a charming laissez-faire about life. She wanted nothing special. She enjoyed being ordinary, unaffected by the exploitations of cunning marketers who kept her peers in the constant throes of needing more.

I glanced over at her desk and was struck by the calendar hanging on her bulletin board. It was turned to the same month and year: May, 1994. I was in the same place, at the same time . . . and yet . . .

"Janie, where is your grandmother?" I barked with such urgency that it startled her.

She turned and looked at me quizzically.

"Mom? You dropped her off at the church this morning. Remember?"

I immediately recalled doing it. I was confused.

"Mom, are you OK? You look a little pale. Everything's going to be OK. You know that, right?"

Across her bookshelves were framed pictures of Noah, Jed the dog, and me. Seeing Noah's likeness with his arms wrapped around me, took my breath away. He had been my first love, and it was true, as he had promised, he never stopped loving me.

Sadly, in this "space" or "universe," or "different path," or " *'what if* scenario"—whatever you want to call it—Noah and I had separated several weeks earlier. We had been trying our best to make our marriage work and had finally come to grips with what we both knew as early as two years into it: Life was not as we had imagined it would be.

Noah had tried to get his degree, but he couldn't keep up with his classes and work two jobs. Meanwhile, all of his single friends had moved on to universities and into young adulthood without him. Noah—married and with a daughter—was forced to grow up too fast, and too soon.

Noah and I had moved into a second story, two-bedroom apartment shortly after our small wedding in the chapel up the road. Noah had taken a job working at a marine shop in Elkton and filled in, when he could, at my father's hardware store. My mom babysat Janie during the gap between when I had to leave for work—waitressing in the same diner where I had worked before giving birth—and when Noah would arrive home. Noah was then left with the evening duties: feeding, bathing, and putting Janie down for the night.

Noah and I believed we were happy, at first. Everything had happened so fast, relatively speaking. We had not had the time to catch our breaths or think about what else we could have been doing with our time had we not become such young parents. I only knew that our dreams always seemed farther out of reach than the "day before and the day before that," and so on.

We had tried to avoid a scandal by marrying quickly. However, his mother and father would not attend the wedding. That certainly raised everyone's suspicions. Then, when I began showing, it seemed the town of North East held its breath, waiting to know the birthdate that would end their skepticism. My parents, on the other hand, smiled bravely through our quiet wedding ceremony and state of pregnancy.

Noah's parents, especially his mother, continued the claim that our hasty plan was going to ruin Noah's life. They disowned us, and their first grandchild. Noah eventually acknowledged his losses. Despite our recent separation, I still had every reason to believe that he remained committed to the promises he had made to me, and to Janie.

I used to gaze into my sundial in those heartbreaking days and wonder where its healing powers had gone.

Noah and I were just scraping by in those early years, and we weren't having much luck saving for a house. Then, Noah's Jeep began costing us more money than new car payments. However, we were cash poor and couldn't come up with the down payment for a new car. Our only family vehicle—aside from Noah's motorcycle—was soon on its last legs. We finally broke down, before it did, and bought a used Ford station wagon. It was a bargain, but it was also a gas-guzzler and Noah was constantly under the hood trying to keep it running. Diapers and formula weren't cheap either, and our rent increased every year as North East began its transformation into a summer destination. Other than that, I was hopeful that our life would one day get better.

"Always the optimist," Noah would say when I tried to paint a brighter picture. But the colors were fading fast and life seemed to be outpacing us.

Noah increasingly missed his family. He missed his little brother who was now in middle school. (Thomas, as it turns out, was a "mistake," too.) Noah missed spending holidays with his larger extended family. He had many cousins whom I had never met. Mostly, he regretted that his parents were missing out on getting to know their wonderful granddaughter.

As money got tighter, our arguments escalated quicker, became fiercer, and more frequent. One night, in the heat of battle, Noah said what I had known all along: He wished that he had gone on to school, perhaps closer to home, and had been a better provider for us. He blamed himself . . . and deep inside, I'm sure he blamed me, too.

It hurt. It cut like a dull serrated knife being pulled across tender flesh until ripping through, allowing the mistakes of life to gush out of a ragged wound. Worse yet, he didn't walk it back or show any remorse for saying it. Instead, he walked out the door, not returning until well after midnight, stinking of beer and cigarettes. Despite his belated apologies and pleading, Noah did not sleep in our bed that night. The next day, my day off, Noah did not return home from work until well after dinner, around ten o'clock. I was worried sick, yet afraid to call my dad and ask if perhaps Noah had stopped by the store to pick up some extra hours. I wanted to protect my husband's pride and not have our situation upset my parents. And I didn't want to explore the limits of my parents' forgiveness either. So, I didn't make the call.

Noah and I had been clashing over what now seems like the most ridiculous things: How much did I spend on groceries? How much did he spend in the bars when he did go out with his buddies? How much did that new flannel shirt cost? I have to work a double at the diner on Saturday. Can you watch Janie? You didn't tell me you were going fishing with the guys on Saturday. Dammit, how much is that flat tire going to cost us? This would not have happened if . . . and the list went on and on.

I could tell that at some point in this place—in this reflection of *what if*—that Noah no longer craved being around me as he used to. However, I couldn't tell you if it was because he thought less of me, or less of himself. The arguments had become predictable, though. He was tired, and probably tired of me. When I found out that he was finding consolation in conversations with a barfly at a local tavern, I packed up Janie and the dog, and moved back in with my parents.

When I had settled back into my mother's house, I took the sundial down to the beach and launched it into the river.

Anyway, that night, Noah had come home to an empty apartment and found the note I had left on the kitchen counter.

"Noah,
I can't do this anymore.
Janie, Jed, and I will be at my parents' for a while.
Love, Faith"

Yes, I had signed it with "Love" because I did love him. Through it all—on this alternate journey of *"what if"*—I had never stopped loving Noah McKenna. My love for him never diminished by any measure. Never.

Just as Janie had said, her best friend Darla drove down the gravel drive and Jed began barking wildly to announce the arrival of his buddy. (Any friend of Janie's was a friend of Jed's, especially if they knew how to give belly rubs.) Like a respectable young lady, Darla came to the door, knocked, and waited for me to invite her in.

"You know, Darla, you don't have to wait outside, just come on in. You're family here."

"Thank you, Mrs. McKenna."

(Mrs. McKenna . . . a name I certainly cherished.)

"So, where are you two off to today?" I asked laced with a dash of suspicion, recalling my own antics at that age.

"Oh, I thought we'd stop by my brother's garage. He's fixing up an old sixty-five Mustang, a real sweet car. Then, maybe the three of us will go grab something to eat," Darla answered.

"Your brother, eh?"

"Yes. Josh is the boss when it comes to cars."

"Does he race?" I asked, hoping the answer was no. Seemed as though everyone in Cecil County with a muscle car was into drag racing.

"Yes! He knows everyone at Cecil County Dragway!"

"Hmmm . . ." I didn't know how to respond, fearing that Darla and Janie might get into trouble—or worse—in a car with someone who enjoyed driving too fast. Someone who might test the limits. My limits.

"Don't worry, Mom," Janie laughed as she entered the small living room. "Josh is a perfect gentleman and a safe driver."

Great . . . she's already been in a car with him.

"Well, stay off the track. Got it?"

I could see that Darla was a little uneasy at my remark, but Janie was clearly smirking. Fortunately, my daughter knew how to take my anxious suspicions in stride.

"I could take him, Mom! We'll soup up the station wagon and I'll wipe Josh clean off the rails!" Janie teased, an obvious poke at my worst fears.

"Ugh," I groaned in protest. "Have a good time and be safe," I said as I hugged and kissed her on her forehead. "And behave!" I directed toward both of them.

As soon as Darla's car disappeared up the dirt drive, my heart sank.

Janie. She's absolutely beautiful. She has her father's wide blue eyes and my strawberry blond hair. She also has my sense of adventure: a reason for concern, that's for sure.

Noah and I had—or would have—created a beautiful creature.

And like the changing tides, my daughter rolled out with her best friend.

Feeling uneasy in the quiet house, I sat down and preoccupied myself for the next several hours going through photo albums and reliving memories that I would have had . . . *or did have?* Tattered books with pages of old photographs of happier times. There was an entire album dedicated to Janie's first year. Pages filled with her being held by Noah and me. I studied the proud smiles on our faces. We appeared to be a happy trio in front of the camera.

Look at us!

Our smiles portrayed the giddiness of new parents, fearful of what the baby was going to do or needed in the next moment.

"Quick, snap the picture before she starts crying!"

(Emotions welled up in me that I had not known, or could not feel sixteen years before.)

There was even a photo of Janie being held by her Aunt Hope. Neither one looked too happy about it. The thought made me laugh.

I turned the page and was captivated by a photo of my dad holding my sleeping baby Janie. He was completely in awe, not even bothering to look up at the camera. Her tiny fingers were wrapped around his large thumb. My father's endearing love was on full display in that photo before me. In Janie, he would have found something no one else could bring him.

The third photo album was lined with pictures that told the story of Noah, Faith, and Janie McKenna. Our tiny apartment was furnished with secondhand furniture. Toys were scattered about the floor creating an indoor field of landmines that required careful navigation by its barefooted occupants. A highchair was a common prop in many of the pictures. Janie was a sloppy eater who apparently liked to feed herself without the aid of utensils. More food clung to her face and glazed her hair than landed on the bib that scarcely protected her clothes. By the time she was one, Janie had become a ham for the camera lens. It also became obvious that I was the one snapping most of the pictures, for Noah was present and I was absent from most of them.

Noah and Janie were so close. She loved her daddy. Despite his dogged tiredness from working two jobs, Noah always had time for his daughter. Several photos included Janie and Noah snuggled together on a worn sofa for a rare afternoon cuddle nap. The resemblance between the two of them was uncanny. Many more showed Noah on the floor playing with his little girl, her stuffed animals and other age appropriate learning toys surrounding them and creating quite a bit of clutter.

Occasionally, I would come across a photo that someone had snapped of the three of us during a holiday or family event. One or both of us was always wrangling Janie, trying to get her to sit still and smile for the camera in the midst of all the excitement.

One photograph, in particular, caught my eye: our first wedding anniversary. Noah, in the only suit that he owned, and I, wearing a dress—something I rarely do, even to this day—were out for an evening alone. Just the two of us. We were seated at a small table with high back chairs, a white linen tablecloth, fine china, and wine glasses half full. Noah was leaning into me with his arm around my shoulder. We looked exhausted, but content; stressed, but relaxed; weary, but we had each other. Yes, I had loved Noah like no other. We had traveled through fire and ice together.

Our separation would be only temporary, I was sure of it.

It wasn't long before the tide changed and drew me toward the dock. Withdrawing the sundial from my pocket, I instinctively knew that it was time to leave and return to the life that I had chosen.

CHAPTER FOUR

FAITH

At this point, if you have no desire to understand my belief in things unseen, you may want to close up this story, for I am about to tell you how I came to trust all that I had just witnessed and how two completely different choices can be reconciled.

If you wish to know, stay the course.

* * *

So we unwittingly say, "The sun comes up in the morning and sets in the evening." But I'm sure you know that in reality the earth revolves around our sun. We speak in terms of how we perceive things from our vantage point, which is rarely a true representation of how the universe actually works. We even talk about how the sun "moves across the sky" or how it "changes position" from one season to the next. That's how we "see" it, even though we know the scientific facts dictate otherwise.

The moon revolves around the earth at twenty-three hundred miles per hour, and yet, on a clear night, we can lie still and gaze up at it while it hangs seemingly motionless in the dark sky. And, on cloudy nights, we cannot view the moon or the stars, yet we know, in reality, they are there. They are just "unseen."

For centuries we've known the earth is round, so we have no qualms about sailing beyond the site of land. We have built technology to bring us back to safe harbor without visibility by the naked eye.

Because of science and nature's repeated patterns and order, we've learn to trust that which we cannot see, even when it is difficult to understand, even when it's bigger than our imaginations, like the universe and all its intra- and interdependencies. We've learned to trust the forces that hold it together, even though we cannot see or fathom the immensity of it all.

Trust, as such, is an action that is grounded in faith.

Well, I'm jumping ahead of myself here, because to be honest with you, at the time, I had no idea what had just happened to me. I was not about to fully trust anything, even though I had just experienced the most significant moment in my life. I had seen my daughter, the one I had given up. I had held her, smelled her, heard her voice, and tasted her skin when I kissed her. Even if it was a dream, it was real to me. I spoke with her. She responded to me. I was in her presence and she was in mine. What had happened to me felt just as real as Charlie and Maddie back in Seattle with their father. I could not see them, but I knew they were there and that they were safe.

My heart was exploding with unspeakable joy . . . and indescribable sorrow. I will never find the words to explain how two competing emotions of such extremes could possibly co-exist within me at the same time without ripping my heart wide open.

As you can imagine, at the time, I was also concerned about losing my grip on reality. So I called Tyler in a concealed panic. I had to make sure that I had fully "returned" and that everything was "in place." It was around lunchtime in Seattle. Tyler assured me that everyone was fine. Though I believe I had aroused his suspicions with my quick interrogation. I tried to matter-of-factly convince him that I just wanted to hear his voice.

The remainder of the afternoon and evening, I walked around in a daze. I didn't want the knowledge of— and the passion for—Janie to leave me. I was troubled about the way things had turned out for Noah and me, yet I had been so excited to meet the one good thing that *had* come from us.

Wait . . . *had, or would have?*

Mom had a late afternoon doctor's appointment and I was needed to drive her. Otherwise, I'm sure I would have returned to the boathouse within the hour. I was like a cat that could not walk away from a frantic moth.

On the drive up Route 272, I had to ask my mom if she had ever had a similar experience, though I had to make sure she would not think me crazy for asking, if she had not.

"Mom, have you ever seen things that really don't exist?"

"What?"

"You know, like, have you ever seen something like a . . . I don't know . . ."

"Like what?"

"I can't quite describe it . . . like something that really isn't there . . . or shouldn't be there."

"You mean like a vision or an apparition?"

"Yeah, something like that, but really seems as real as real can be."

"Can't say that I have."

That was all she said. She never bothered to ask why I wanted to know. If Charlie or Maddie had asked me that kind of a question, my curiosity would have gone sky-high and I'd want to know why they had asked.

Seated in the waiting room, I studied the other individuals surrounding us, wondering if they, too, had had an experience similar to mine.

Am I the only one?

My wonderings went back to Janie. What was she doing at that very moment? Was she still out with Darla and Darla's brother? He could have been a nice young man, but you can't trust them once they come of age. Compared to most, Noah was a saint, and look how far we had gone. Admittedly, I was always moving faster than Noah was, sending him signals that indicated I needed more. Noah was a rare breed, though; there's no denying that.

Janie has Noah's good looks, but what if she inherited my libido? God help her. God help us ...

Mom was called back to see the doctor, and I was left to sit alone with four strangers. One was browsing through a May edition of People Magazine with Meg Ryan on the cover and the title "The 50 Most Beautiful People in the World, 1994." Two others were whispering and having a good chuckle as they watched the famed mathematician, John Nash, on CNN discussing the possibility of humans living on Mars.

Life elsewhere ... Now there's a thought.

But, nothing seemed out of the ordinary for anyone seated in the waiting room. Apparently, I was the only person in the world who was recovering from an out-of-body experience. Did I appear restless, or half insane? Because I was certainly working hard to cover it. To top it off, the longer I sat there, the more I could feel paranoia setting in, as if I had ascertained something that the rest of the world could not, or that I had gone completely mad.

After dinner that evening, Mom suggested that we have coffee down on the dock.
"I'm not so sure that's a good idea."
"Oh? Don't be silly. It's a nice warm evening. It will be the perfect way to end the day."
"I don't know, Mom ..."
"Well, I'm going, whether you're coming or not."
Mom could be very stubborn at times. It was better that I go along with her than allow her to walk down the uneven bank on her own. If she fell again, my sister would be all over me about letting her go alone. More importantly, I didn't know what had happened down there on my last visit.

"OK, then. Let me take the coffees down first, and then I'll come back and get you."

"I'm not an invalid, Faith. I do this every day."

"I know, but . . ."

"You can't stay here forever. I need to be able to take care of myself."

"I don't think you're ready to walk down the bank by yourself."

"Stop, Faith. I'm going."

"OK . . .OK. Since you're in such a hurry, let me get the coffee started and then we'll walk down together."

I heard the screen door slam behind her. She insisted in striking out on her own while I was pouring water into the old percolator.

Dammit!

I immediately stopped what I was doing and ran after her.

"Wait, Mom! You're incorrigible, you know that?" I caught up to her and stayed by her side, keeping pace with her slow, unsteady footing.

"See," she boasted, "I'm fine. There's no reason for you girls to make such a fuss."

Little did she know that my real concern was lurking down on the dock, in the boathouse.

Could what happened to me happen to anyone else who got too close?

Walking past the outer wall of the boathouse, I was on high alert. I wanted to grab my mother's arm to make sure she wasn't pulled away without me.

Or, what if I suddenly disappeared?

I chuckled.

She might not even notice! Not funny.

Mom made it to her favorite seat at the glass top table and then plopped down. She was out of breath.

"There," she huffed. "Satisfied?"

"Yes, Mom." I looked around to make sure nothing was out of order.

OK. No spinning. That's good.

The interior of the boathouse was dark.

Whew, that's another good sign.

OK, Mom. Don't go anywhere. I'll be right back with our coffees."

"And where do you think I'm going to go?"

"And, NO SMOKING!"

She grunted and pulled out her cigarettes.

I should have known.

It took forever for the percolator to finish up. I stood at the window and watched to make sure nothing suspicious was going on down at the dock. All seemed quiet. With the absence of a breeze, the smoke from my mother's cigarette was rising straight up. The river was calm and from the house, the water looked like a mirror reflecting the high wispy clouds above it; a canvas painted in hues of pinks, oranges, blues, and violets. Soon enough it would turn dark and the tree frogs and crickets would begin their nighttime serenades.

Mom and I sat facing the western sky, watching the sun rapidly lose its grip on the opposite bank of the river. Uncharacteristically, Mom shared a memory as she flicked a second cigarette butt into the water.

"Your father and I rarely got to enjoy sunsets like this. He worked so hard so the rest of us could enjoy life."

"I know, Mom. He would have been very happy to see us here."

"Yes, he would."

That was all she said.

Her cigarette butt floated motionless beside the dock where she had flicked it.

Slack tide.

"Mom . . ." I tiptoed very carefully around the question I was about to ask. "Have you ever felt like Dad was here, like he was right here?"

"No. Of course not."

"You don't ever get the sense that he is nearby?"

"No."

"Oh," I acknowledged, clearly disappointed.

Again, that was it. There was no way to take it any further without her thinking I was trying to dredge up some kind of unnecessary misery. She had shared her one happy thought and I knew it was best to leave it at that.

After Mom had gone off to bed, I waited another thirty minutes and then sneaked back down to the boathouse. Having polished off a glass of wine and two more chapters of a book, I was more than ready. Making my way down the darkened path shortly after ten o'clock, I only rolled my ankle once on an unfamiliar root that was exposed above the ground. Nary a curse word escaped my mouth, even though it hurt like hell.

Glad to be on the flat surface of the dock, I straightened up and walked like a normal person. The boathouse was highlighted by the light of the full moon, making everything appear larger than it actually was. I peered in the window by the door. It was quiet and dark inside. Feeling safe, yet curious, I opened the door as far as I could without scraping it along the dock. Nothing. Nothing happened. No tingles. No lightheadedness. Just darkness and high anxiety.

Could it all have been just my imagination?

With conflicted hopes, I stood inside the boathouse and waited. Not even a bit of nostalgia pricked my heart. I stood in fidgety silence for several long seconds, something less than a minute. I heard nothing. I felt nothing other than the musty air clinging to my skin and clogging my nasal passages.

Slightly defeated, I gave up and walked back out onto the dock. On the opposite bank of the river at Carpenter Point, lights formed the same patterns they had decades ago when I was growing up. They were dimmer on this particular night because of the bright illumination of the full moon outshining them as it cast a long glaze across the choppy ripples of the water. If I had had a flashlight, I could have easily picked up Green Can #9, a channel marker that was directly out from our dock. I knew exactly where it was and could faintly see it in the bright moonlight. The other channel markers, one north and one south of the green can, continued flashing red, at different intervals. Everything was the same. Nothing had changed.

Reminiscing upon the late nightscape, I was also reminded that Noah now lived nearby, in the parsonage beside the chapel. My mom may have even been to his house. After all, she was a member of a small church, in a small town. It was a place where everyone knew everyone's secrets. Or, so they thought.

Since the last time I had seen Noah, he had married Chrissy. I know this because Mom had always called me in Seattle to announce the new milestones of their relationship, probably to suggest that everything had turned out for the best, for both of us. I remember how shortly after my dad's funeral, Mom had called to tell me that Noah had a girlfriend. A year later, she sent me an article announcing their engagement. I cried.

How could he love anyone the way he loved me?

Mom actually attended the wedding service at the chapel. Perhaps this was her way of absolving herself of guilt. Still, I also believed that in some strange way, she wished that I had kept the baby and married Noah.

To date, to the best of my knowledge and because Mom has not announced it, Noah and Chrissy have not had any children. It was probably only a matter of time.

Janie . . .
Noah and I would have named her "Janie."

In a disappointed stupor, I made my way back up to the house. The dew was beginning to settle and everything was turning damp. Before the end of the day, I called Tyler, again, and spoke with the girls. They had kept up our family routines and everyone was doing fine. I was missing them terribly and felt as though I had somehow cheated on them by "revisiting" other past *possibilities*. Being back on the North East River made avoiding these "reflections of *'what if?'* " nearly impossible.

The following day, Mom asked me to take her to the Acme supermarket located on our end of town. It was a quick drive and the morning was off to a good start, until we turned into aisle three. Who do we run into but Chrissy McKenna.

"Oh, Chrissy!" my mother swooned. "I'd like you to meet my daughter, Faith."

"Hi, Faith," Chrissy said as she extended her hand.

"Hello, Chrissy. I believe we've met before . . . at my father's funeral," I acknowledged awkwardly. Her hand was soft and frail.

"Yes, I remember. Noah was very fond of your father. He still speaks of him occasionally. How many years has it been?"

"Nine, almost ten."

"If you remember," my mom jumped in, "Faith was pregnant at the time. She now has two girls! Charlotte is nine and Madison is seven."

"Oh, congratulations!" Chrissy said with animated sincerity.

"Do you and Noah have any children yet?" I asked. The question just popped out of my mouth without forethought.

"No, no children."

A very long pause followed and then I made a feeble attempt at smoothing over my insensitivity.

"Oh, well, there's plenty of time for that," I maintained, as if I needed to console her, which probably just made my glib remark even more awkward.

Are you in town for a visit?" she asked politely, redirecting our conversation, thankfully.

"Yes, I'm helping my mom for a couple of weeks while Hope and Drew are away."

That's when my mom decided to hijack the conversation.

"Why don't you and Noah stop by for lunch one day while Faith is still in town?" my mother suggested as if this would be the loveliest thing ever.

"Mom," I somewhat snarled, "I'm sure Noah and Chrissy are very busy."

"Oh, no. I think that would be very nice," Chrissy responded sweetly.

"How about tomorrow?" Mom insisted.

I was completely aghast. Speechless at this point.

"OK, I'll check with Noah, but unless you hear from us otherwise, we'll be there at noon. What can we bring?"

In the background, Mom and Chrissy worked out the menu while I stood in shock, right there in aisle three, beside the mixers.

I need a drink right now . . .

The remainder of the day was rather dull. A quick rain shower passed through in the afternoon. Nothing substantial, just enough to make everything wet and miserable. By the time the sun made another full appearance, it was time to prepare dinner. Mom wanted pasta, so I made a large batch of chicken fettuccini.

As it turned out, I must have been famished because I ate more than my fair share. After I had scarfed down a second helping, I was pretty sure I could feel my stomach overlapping the waistband of my shorts.

"Mom, I'm going for a walk while it's still light out. I'll do the dishes when I get back. Is that OK with you?" I asked as I got up from the table and stacked our dishes on the kitchen counter beside the sink.

"Sure. That's fine. Though, I can do them myself, you know," Mom grumbled.

I made my way back to my old bedroom and changed my shoes, filled a water bottle on my way back through the kitchen, and was out the door in less than five minutes.

The evening air was unseasonably hot and humid. It had been a week of near record-breaking temperatures, just shy of a heat wave. A late day thunderstorm appeared to be building in the west. I would have to keep an eye on the weather.

I started up Riverside Drive, making my way toward Route 272. I planned to turn south toward the Turkey Point Lighthouse. I had no idea how far I'd get before the first thunder clap, or sunset, whichever came first. Then, I might have to sprint for home. Route 272, a.k.a. Turkey Point Road, was a smooth macadam road with a wide shoulder, which always made for a nice morning or evening run. Plus, on this end of the peninsula, there was very little traffic.

NOAH

Nigel's parents had called and begged me to meet them at Turkey Point Lighthouse. Their son was perched on the rail of the gallery overlooking the junction of three rivers and was now threatening to jump if anyone approached him. Chrissy wasn't due home for another half hour, so I would have to go it alone.

* * *

Nigel and I had recently formed a special bond. Long story short, he was eighteen and a senior in high school. Known to few, Nigel was gay. At the time, he had not "come out." Unfortunately, however, he had been *found out*; caught on a yacht at one of the local marinas. If I didn't know better, I'd say a group of high school classmates had set a trap to catch him in the act. Word spread fast and the poor lad was quickly labeled and ostracized by his peers. In the midst of his distress, his only remaining friend in school, and in the world, had begged him to see me before doing anything rash.

Thank God, Chrissy was home when our first meeting took place. I will never forget it as long as I live. Nigel's friend, Emily, delivered him to our house, and left as soon as the introductions were complete. Chrissy then ushered Nigel into our living room and seated him in her favorite chair.

"Please, Nigel, have a seat. Would you like some tea, a soda, or some ice water?" she asked as if she were entertaining any other houseguest or visiting parishioner.

"No, thank you, ma'am," Nigel responded politely.

"Mrs. McKenna. You can call me Mrs. McKenna."

Before anything further was said, we allowed time for Nigel to acclimate. He sat quiet and pensive, head down, perhaps trying to think through why he had given in to the pleas of his only friend.

We knew why he had been sent to us. We had been clued in.

When it felt right, Chrissy broke the ice.

"Nigel, your friend, Emily, attends our church. She believes Pastor Noah might be able to help you."

"Mrs. McKenna, unless you and Pastor McKenna can make me disappear, there isn't much you can do for me," Nigel muttered, keeping his head down.

"Why on earth would a good-looking young man like you want to disappear? In several weeks' time, you'll graduate and you'll have your whole life ahead of you," Chrissy encouraged.

"There's no life out there for me," Nigel said, remaining hunched over in the chair. He looked totally defeated.

"Isn't there something you'd like to do after graduation?"

Nigel drew his eyes up, but his body remained curled in defeat, his forearms resting on his knees with his hands folded in front of him.

"Mrs. McKenna, I'm sure Emily meant well by bringing me here. But I'm not sure what you can do for me. I should probably go."

"Wait," I interrupted, thrusting my hand up to halt his exit. "I know this can't be easy for you. But you're here, so why not let us know if there is some way we can help? Let's start with why Emily brought you here."

"Everybody knows, Pastor McKenna. No use beating around the bush. Go ahead. Tell me I'm going to hell, even though Emily assured me that you won't try to beat me straight with a Bible."

"Please, call me Noah, or Pastor Noah, if need be. But the point is: Emily is right. I am not here to beat you over the head with a Bible. What good would that do you, or anyone else for that matter? I—of all people—know that I am the last person on earth with the right to condemn you for anything that you've done."

"Sure, you can say that all you want, but I know what the church thinks of me. I've been told many times over what God thinks of me, and people like me. I've been shouted at, threatened repeatedly, shoved, kicked, spat upon . . . you name it. And I know some of those kids, and their parents, attend your church."

The thought of my parishioners, no matter what their age, behaving in such a way, made me sick. Remorse and guilt crept in on all sides.

Have I not taught them anything?

"That doesn't make it right, or excuse their behavior. You think Christians are a righteous lot? They're not. And they're wrong for treating you in the ways you've just described," I continued, heartsick.

"I'm gay, Pastor Noah. Did you know that? "

"So?"

"So, that makes me the scourge of the earth. I'm a . . . an abomination."

"I know that's what some people want you to believe, Nigel, but I don't happen to agree."

"Well, they claim they're quoting from scripture. They've even hurled Bible verses at me to prove their point."

"Unfortunately, people love to throw around lines of scripture with no context around them, making them weapons to justify their own fears, which usually end up driving some misguided agenda. Do you believe their insults and threats are what God has intended for you?"

"I don't know. Maybe? I've looked some of them up, and it sure sounds like it."

"Well, I don't believe that's God's intent. Their interpretations are being driven by their fears. For example: Everybody's real keen on John 3:16. 'For God so loved the world that he sent his only son, that whosoever believes in him shall not die, but have everlasting life.' Sound familiar?"

"Yes."

"Well, what they forgot is what comes immediately after, which is God's important explanation and reasoning for doing what he did. 'For God sent his son not to *condemn* the world, but to *save* it.' Now, that's the exact opposite of what most people want you to believe. Isn't it?"

"I don't know."

He came to *save the world*, Nigel. That's *everyone*. If that weren't true, then we're all condemned. Why would He send his son to suffer and die if he were going to let one soul perish? If God wants victory, believe me, He will have it. Do you believe that, Nigel?"

"That means He will have to kill me."

"No, Nigel. It means that through His Son, He forgives all of us. You . . . and me."

For the first time, Nigel sat up a little taller.

"So God's going to beat the gay out of me?" he asked.

"No, Nigel. The beating has already taken place. His Son took the beating for all of us. Everyone. Without exception."

"Come on, Pastor," Nigel said, raising his voice in frustration, "that doesn't change anything. I'm still gay."

"Yes. And I still commit sins everyday."

"What sins do you commit? Do you live a sinful life? Do you know what it's like to live in the shadows: to be isolated from everyone? Do you know what it's like to have people look at you like you're a freak, or that your life is a threat to their children? Like you're diseased, or you've made some sick choice? Do you know what it feels like to think that maybe you deserve the beating? I doubt it.

"I've watched all my classmates date and go to prom. Hold hands with their girlfriends. Talk smack in the locker room or after school, boasting about their conquests, one outdoing the other. Then they look at me like I'm a piece of shhhh. . . Sorry.

"I've tried, off and on for years, to be like everyone else. I've even prayed about it. Nothing's going to change. I know that now.

"I have to look behind my back everywhere I go."

Chrissy jumped in and asked two questions as if their answers were plain as day.

"Nigel, sin is sin. No one sin is greater than another in the eyes of God. Therefore, I'd say all sin is an abomination, as you called it. Do you think Pastor Noah went through his whole day without committing a single sin? Tell him, Noah. What sin did you commit today?"

I was caught off guard, again, and clearly unprepared. Should I name something that would *sound* equally as abominable as Nigel's sexual orientation? My brain scrambled for some recollection that I could share. Chrissy came to the rescue . . . or not.

"Pastor Noah got a girl pregnant when he was eighteen. Isn't that right, Noah?"

I was floored, and even a little angry, that she dared to share that part of my life, of Faith's life—a well-guarded secret.

Chrissy and I have no secrets, but this was something I had not dared to share openly with my congregants, or anyone else for that matter, let alone a stranger. Mrs. Cuthbertson obviously knew, but she was not going to open up about it either. I assumed the miscarriage was not something she wanted talked about.

"Yes," I answered ashamedly.

"Go ahead, and tell Nigel that when a beautiful woman passes by your imagination doesn't wander, not even for a split second."

"Chrissy!" I replied, unintentionally scolding her. It was a first.

Where is she going with this?

"Go ahead, Noah. You're a man. Tell Nigel," Chrissy implored.

"OK . . . sure."

"Right," Chrissy confirmed. "We're all human and we're all full of sin. Not a one of us is without blemish or fault. It's that simple. It's just that as broken people, we like to redeem ourselves by saying that some sin is more damning than others. The Bible is very specific that no sin is greater than another. In fact, the only sin that is unforgivable is blaspheming God, or in other words, denying His existence."

"Mrs. McKenna, with all due respect, you have no idea what my life is like. I don't know how you can equate your lives with what I'm going through. What I live with every day."

"You're right, Nigel, I haven't a clue what your life is like. If I saw you and another young man together, I'd probably stare, just like everyone else. I might even forget myself and whisper about the two men who just walked by and what a waste it was that two such handsome men were gay. There's a full day's worth of gossip there. Did you know that gossip is a sin? So you see, that would make me no better than you or anyone else on this earth. I am no better or worse than you, and neither is Pastor Noah, or any other Christian or human being. Sometimes, Christians are the most self-righteous people I know. Did you know Pastor Noah and I had sex before we were married?"

Chrissy had just betrayed our deepest secret for the sake of this young man. I didn't know whether to be angry with her or proud of her. So much for "no one has to know."

Nigel looked a little stunned at Chrissy's unveiling.

"Don't worry, Noah," Chrissy assured as she patted my knee, "If need be, I'll confess that I seduced you."

Yes, Nigel was stunned momentarily—and so was I. Chrissy's transparency had allowed Nigel to see us as real people: imperfect and flawed. Carnal sinners, just like everyone else. Just like him. Inside, I was seething.

Nigel's demeanor shifted, as did his body.

Chrissy continued.

"Christians can be hypocrites, Nigel. We're no better than anyone else. Wouldn't you say? You experience it every day. Yet, Jesus' one command is to 'love God with all your heart and love your neighbor as yourself.' Is that what you're experiencing from your Christian friends, Nigel?"

Nigel's eyes widened. Dare he answer with what he truly thought? What he had been experiencing in his young life?

"No . . ." he responded cautiously, as if testing the water. "Except for Emily."

"Yes, Emily is a good friend. See? So, if you were to sit in our sanctuary during a Sunday service, you would be surrounded by people no better than you, no more or less loved by God than you."

"It's not that simple, Mrs. McKenna. What you did, or do, is socially acceptable, and you *did* marry, after all. I live in this body. I'm a freak, someone who doesn't belong. I've lost all my friends, except for Emily, and I'm not sure how much longer she'll be able to put up with the bullying she receives just because she stands by me. I'm living with threats, and I'm sure she will soon, too, if she hasn't received them already. And what about my poor mother? Her friends are now telling her that she has to do something about her gay son."

Nigel was allowing us into his world—as much as we could possibly understand. Enough for us to have sympathy for Nigel and regret the way he was being treated by others, and by members of our own church family. My anger with Chrissy's transparency slowly subsided. She had managed to present Nigel with the reality of all human brokenness by way of our own admissions. She exposed things about us that weren't as obvious or discoverable, if you will, as Nigel's gay life. How daunting it must be for him at his age. I couldn't imagine the courage it took for him to get up every day and go to school, surrounded by the very people who were displaying such hate directed toward him.

I decided to dive a little deeper.

"Nigel, we know what happened at the marina. I'm very sorry for the actions of others. . . . This person that you were with, do you *love* him?"

"Yes, I think I do. He's a very important man, Pastor Noah. So none of this can get back to his family or his clients."

"His family?" Chrissy and I asked in unison.

"Yes," Nigel answered, now showing real regret and shame.

FAITH

I had just arrived at the intersection of Turkey Point Road when a Jeep slammed on its brakes, skidding past me. Then it backed up. Frightened, I turned to run back to the house.

"FAITH! WAIT! I thought that was you, I'd recognize that gait and ponytail anywhere. Where are you headed?"

I stopped in my tracks, horrified and out of breath. I knew that voice. It was the very same one that I had listened to in church that past Sunday.

"Noah, what the hell?"

"Hurry up, hop in," he yelled out through the passenger side.

Two state troopers, an ambulance, and a fire truck flew by, sirens blaring. I covered my ears.

"Hop in," Noah yelled again, more assertively.

"Hop in? Why?"

"Just get in. I don't have time to explain."

Noah seemed out of sorts, something urgent was afoot. Against my better judgment—of which I exercised none at the time—I jumped into Noah's Jeep.

"What's up?" I asked as I buckled up.

Noah hit the accelerator and sped toward the southern tip of the peninsula.

"I have a friend who needs some coaxing down off the lighthouse."

"Coaxing? The lighthouse?"

"Yeah, he's on the rail refusing to come down."

"And you picked me up because?"

"Because . . . I might need a wingman . . . er . . . person."

"Where's Chrissy?"

"She's not due home for another couple of hours. This can't wait."

Before I knew it, we were on the dirt trail leading up to the lighthouse. Riding in the open Jeep, soaked in sweat from my fast-paced walk, the dust was sticking to me as if it were being sucked up by a damp mop. So gross. The emergency vehicles had gone before us leaving Noah to navigate the ragged terrain through flying debris still airborne from the spinning tires ahead of us. The gritty haze did not slow Noah down, though, and we were getting bounced around inside the Jeep like a call to customer service at a large corporate bank. Reaching the end of the trail, the Jeep slid to a halt and Noah jumped out.

"Come on!" he yelled, taking off at a sprint.

I raced up behind him, zig-zagging through the parked emergency vehicles and their flashing lights.

Sure enough, there was a young man perched up on the gallery rail of the lighthouse overlooking the juncture of the three rivers.

"NIGEL, YOU PICKED A FINE TIME TO PULL THIS STUNT!" Noah shouted upward. "I WAS JUST ABOUT TO SIT DOWN TO DINNER!"

The young man turned his head, saw Noah, and then looked back toward the water.

Noah pulled up beside a couple who were about ten years older than us. Just from the bits and pieces of conversation that I could pick up, I assumed the woman was the young man's mother. She and several State Troopers shared a brief exchange with Noah. One of the Troopers nodded an "OK" to whatever had been discussed.

"NIGEL!" Noah shouted up toward the lighthouse gallery, "I'M COMING UP!"

"Wait here," Noah instructed me. "And ask those guys to turn off all those flashing lights . . . please."

I could hear Noah running up the wooden lighthouse stairs. Spiraling upward, his footsteps faded away as he neared the top. And then, seconds later, he appeared standing next to the young man known as "Nigel."

Noah eventually sat up on the gallery rail alongside Nigel. Their two little figures motionless as they held on to the rail, chatting like there was nothing unusual going on.

Just two guys talking about baseball or something else just
as meaningless. They were far enough up, that none of us
on the ground could hear their conversation or read their
lips or body language. So we were totally in the dark, yet
they held our stares with rapt attention. Nigel and Noah
remained there for a long time, long enough for my neck to
get a crick in it from craning upward. Noah finally came
down from the rail and held his hand out to Nigel. Nigel
took it and hopped off the rail to safety. On the ground,
Nigel's mother let out a weighted sigh and fell against the
chest of the man standing beside her.

Noah and Nigel stayed at the top of the lighthouse
for another thirty minutes, or so. The sun was beginning to
descend more rapidly and a sweaty chill ran down my back.

"What's taking them so long?" Nigel's mother asked
the man holding her.

"With Nigel, it's anyone's guess," the man huffed.

By the time all of the emergency equipment had
vacated the area it was almost dark. At Noah's behest, Nigel
was released into his mother's care, avoiding arrest or a
trip to the hospital for evaluation. (Noah's opinion,
obviously, was highly regarded by the local community.)

Noah and I were left standing, alone, before the
silent lighthouse and its seductive rotating light that
intensified as darkness fell upon the Point. Pronouncing fair
warning to those at sea, the lantern also seemed to be
cautioning me about being alone with this handsome
grown man who was once my young, captivating lover.
That's when Noah suggested that we "sit for a while and
catch up."

Noah and I walked over to the edge of the bank,
right past the warning signs, just as we would have done all
those years ago, and sat in the grass. From our vantage
point atop the hundred-foot bluff, we gazed out across the
juncture of the three rivers—the North East River, The Elk,
and the Susquehanna—that formed the land mass known
as Turkey Point. Everything was the same as I had
remembered, only the trees had grown taller; there were

newer houses built on the far bank of the Elk River; and we had grown older . . . and hopefully wiser.

"What happened up there, Noah?" I needed to ask before we dove into our own personal stories.

"Oh . . . that? Another teenager dealing with growing up in a hypocritical world."

"Oh. How did you get him down?"

"I told him there was One greater than all of us, One who loves him no matter what he's done or who he is. That his life matters to a lot of people, including Chrissy and me."

"And that worked?"

"He's no different than you or me, Faith. He only needed to know that someone believes in him and that things *will* get better. It's not the first time that he and I have had this talk, either. Anyway, he got dumped last night, and he had no one to go to."

"Oh . . . that sucks."

"Yeah, it sucks, alright, but it was probably the best thing to happen to him, in all honesty. It was not the best relationship for him to be in. He's a very nice young man trying to survive in a very ugly world."

Silence fell between us as I recalled our own breakup. Apparently, Noah and I were sharing the same wavelength.

"Faith, speaking of breakups, what happened to us?"

"Noah, you really want to get into this?"

"I've always wondered."

"I lost the baby, Noah. I had all kinds of things going on that I still don't understand to this day. I'd really rather not revisit it."

But, I had revisited it . . . in a very real way.

"Well . . . just know that I'm very sorry for all that I put you through. I never meant to cause you any pain or distress. I never wanted you to go through it alone, but you shut me out. I hope you can believe that I'm sorry. I'm *really* sorry," he repeated.

His sincere sympathies and concern felt so familiar, so intimate and natural that I almost lost my way.

"Are you happy, Faith?"

"Yes. And you? Are you happy?"

"Yes. And I would be happier if I knew . . . well . . . if I was sure that you survived it all," he stumbled, pulling an errant piece of tall, straw-like grass from the ground.

"Yes . . . I've survived, Noah, though that's a strange way to put it. I've been fine for a long time now. It would probably be best if we didn't open old wounds, though. That tends to leave deeper scars. Agreed?"

Noah nodded, placing the straw in his mouth, just as he used to do.

"Instead, tell me how you got into the ministry? I mean . . ."

"You mean you can't believe I would ever become a pastor?"

"Yeah. How did *that* happen?"

"Uh . . . well, God can take an ordinary person . . . no, a broken nobody, like me . . . and do some pretty unpredictable things."

"God, huh? You're really into this God stuff. It's a real thing for you?"

"Of course it is!" Noah snorted, somewhat incensed by my question. "I was pretty banged up after you rejected me. My freshman year at BU was hell. Unlike you, I didn't recover. I guess that's what makes me pretty pathetic: you had no choice but to face your loss and find a way to endure it. And you did . . . on your own. I didn't fare as well. In fact, it wasn't until I got involved in a campus ministry that I found a way to move through it."

"Wow, you really went off the deep end. Please . . . give me a break." Now I was the one irritated, incensed by his seemingly cavalier remarks, insinuating that I had an easy time of it.

"I'm serious, Faith. The only reason I was able to help Nigel tonight is because I understand him. Well . . . not completely understand him. But, he's got a lot going on and he is in the thick of it. I know what it's like to feel totally abandoned."

I had no idea what to say. And if I'm going to be perfectly honest about it, I was a little ticked off that he was perhaps implying that his suffering was justifiably equal to, or worse than, mine.

"So then, somehow, you ended up pastoring a church ... here, of all places."

"Yes, I've always loved it here," Noah said, pulling the grass from his mouth as he looked at me. "And then I met Chrissy." He paused, lost in his thoughts. "You'll love her, Faith."

We just stared at each other. It was a dare to see who would flinch first. Who would be first to admit that perhaps we were not "over it." That we had not, in fact, moved on. I thought about Tyler. I thought about Charlie and Maddie, and their sweet laughs and innocent smiles. I'm sure Noah was thinking of Chrissy, too, and whether or not his life now measured up to what life "could have been."

Noah was first to break the uncomfortable silence.

"I understand we're all getting together for lunch at your mother's house tomorrow."

"Yes, you can thank your wife and my mother for that."

"Well, I'm looking forward to it," Noah crowed.

"Me, too," I responded hoping I didn't sound as half-hearted as I felt.

Noah drove me home. That evening was the first time I had been in a vehicle with him in sixteen years. It was the first time we had not kissed goodnight before I got out of his Jeep at the end of my lane.

Life had become complicated and restless on the banks of the North East River.

That night, long after I had spoken with Tyler and the girls on the phone, I couldn't help but reflect back on watching Noah coax that young man "off the ledge," or what it was like to ride in his open Jeep, with a bright moon peering in and out of the passing trees, or sitting next to him noticing the shadows move across his face as other vehicles passed us by. I remembered the day we had first met: the time he had rescued me and my capsized boat in the channel of the river. Our first kiss. Our nights in the boathouse. Everything came flooding back to me in torrents of mixed emotions.

Was I really OK? Had I truly survived?

I walked back to my old bedroom and grabbed the sundial from the top of my dresser. Turning it over in my hands brought me some comfort, glad that we had been reunited—that shell and me—but I knew I was mourning a deep, perplexing loss.

Long after midnight, I still couldn't find sleep. My restless energy was adamant that I not locate a comfortable position on my old tired mattress. The moon was up and shining brilliantly, illuminating a path to the dock. So, I decided to take a walk down to the water. The lunar nightlight cast shadows of tall oaks across the sloping bank. Up river, a mallard was making a racket about something that it had found displeasing. Its squawking echoed across the smooth surface of the dark water. Occasionally, I heard a fish jump, hoping for a mosquito meal. Lord knows I had donated plenty to that banquet throughout my years.

A leaf drifted down the river—from the right side of the dock to the left—indicating that the tide was moving out. As soon as I rounded the boathouse, sure enough, there was the familiar warm glow coming from within. In some weird way it was exhilarating, like the leeward side of a catamaran sinking into the water as the windward pontoon rises up. I exhaled deeply. My heart began pounding.

OK, this time I am going to figure it out.

I pulled the door open and stepped inside. The sundial flipped out of my hand and fell to the floor.

Shit.

I stooped over to pick it up. Gingerly, I lifted it and peered into the concave spiral of its underside, the warm glow illuminating its transfixing staircase.

As if silently preyed upon, I felt as though something was closing in on me. My vision, already hampered by my surroundings, was narrowing as my body began feeling weightless, yet my feet were solidly planted on the floor of the boathouse. Everything started to accelerate, faster than before. With no sign of stopping and reaching a frightening velocity, I tried to scream, but nothing came out. I had expelled all of the air in my lungs in my failed attempt to call out, and the suffocation rapidly began. It felt like someone had thrown me up against the wall, knocking all of the wind out of me. Still, I remained standing in the middle of the boathouse. Unable to breathe, the interior faded to black—pitch black. The congestion building in my head was unrelenting and the pressure became unbearable. My eyes remained open, though I had lost my sight. I lost all the feeling in my arms and legs, numbness creeping up to my core. Falling. I was falling, but my feet—even though I could no longer acknowledge them—were still standing steadfast on the boathouse floorboards. I was going to crash. I was descending so rapidly, I knew I was going to die once I hit bottom. The floorboards were dropping faster and farther, and I had the sensation of achieving an astronomical speed.

How far I fell, I cannot say. Maybe not at all, for soon my stomach was rising to my throat like a swift elevator ride coming to an end. My hands and feet were painfully tingling and became heavy as my blood began circulating through them once again. My ears were humming. Sight returned to my eyes with a sudden flash. Each time I blinked, my focus improved.

My sinuses were the last to clear, and I was keenly aware that I was still inside the boathouse, but as before, everything was new, clean, and repaired.

I stepped carefully out onto the dock. The sky was still clear; the moon was still as bright as ever, outshining its neighbors in the galaxy; and the mallard was still squawking up river.

Behind me, headlights were coming down the dirt drive toward the house. It was Darla's car, returning with Janie, as promised.

I carefully shoved the sundial into my pocket and made my way up to the house. As I came through the back door, Janie was placing a harness on Jed while Darla held Janie's pillow and sleeping bag under her arm. They were leaving for a sleepover at Darla's.

"Mom!" Janie squealed, excited to see me. "Some kid from high school tried to jump off the lighthouse tonight and Dad talked him down."

I'm sure I looked dumbfounded.

"Are you sure?"

"Yes. Dad was the first person on the scene and word has it that he talked the kid down."

I grabbed the end of the kitchen table, fearing that I might fall over at the news.

"Were you there, Janie? Did you see any of this?"

"No. Some guys came into the garage and told us about it," Janie reported. Then she spoke quietly, as if she was speaking about something illicit. "They said the guy is gay, Mom. Can you believe it? They said that Dad should've let him jump."

"Janie, you shouldn't go around spreading rumors, especially because you weren't there, and you don't know for a fact that what you're saying is true."

"Oh no, these guys know it for a fact, Mrs. McKenna," Darla jumped in. "He's been caught in the act, if you know what I mean," she snickered. "They said he's as queer as a three dollar bill."

Janie gave Darla a shot in the arm.

"Leave the poor kid alone, Darla. My dad did the right thing."

"Of course he did," Darla corrected, realizing that not everyone in the house felt compelled to make fun and carry on about such a thing.

"OK, Mom. We're going to grab some ice cream and Cool Whip and head back to Darla's for a sleepover."

Hearing the words "ice cream," Jed started jumping up and down in rapid succession as if he were a pogo stick.

"See, Darla? He's a smart dog! Smarter than your brother's dumb Chessy."

"Anything is smarter than that dumb dog. I think he ran into one too many walls when he was a pup."

Janie laughed as she scratched Jed behind his ears.

"Why not stay here?" I asked, somewhat disappointed.

"Oh, the Dauber's just got a large screen TV, so we're going to watch a movie there," Janie answered excitedly. "We're taking Jed with us. Mrs. Dauber said it's OK."

"All right, then, I'll see you in the morning," I said, though strangely I knew that wasn't true. I would be gone by morning.

"OK, Mom, we're outta here!"

And just like that, they exited the house.

Silence pervaded the emptiness.

Trying to imagine the earlier scene described by Janie, I envisioned Noah doing what he certainly would have done. Here, in "this place," having married early and feeling deprived of his youth, Noah had joined the local fire company as a volunteer. That explains how he ended up at the lighthouse to rescue the young man.

The remainder of the evening, I lingered on the couch, flipping through some magazines and newspapers. The stories were the same. Mostly, everything was the same. Mostly.

But *"here,"* I missed Noah. I missed our fights and our make-ups. I missed waiting for him to come home late at night, wondering where he had been.

Separated.

"Here," my marital status was "separated."

Should I go out to the tavern to find him?
And what would happen if I did find him? Would he be
upset that I was following him?
What if he was entertaining someone else?
Maybe he's at the apartment. It's still my home, too.
Why shouldn't I be able to go over there? I could say I
stopped by to pick up a book, or something else I had
forgotten.

I grabbed my keys and started out the door.

I can't do this. I can't go chasing after him. Not at this
late hour. Dammit.

No matter what, I couldn't stay in my mother's
house any longer that night, not with Janie gone. So I got
into the car and drove out to Route 272. Without thinking, I
turned left and drove straight to Bay Boat Works where the
"Nauti-lass III" was docked. (Yes, the McKenna family was
now on their third yacht.) There I found Noah's motorcycle
parked alongside a Lincoln. I could only assume the car
belonged to his parents. Fearful someone would recognize
our old station wagon, I drove away.

Noah had returned to his family, and they must have
received him.

Perhaps, it's all for the best.

I didn't know whether I should be happy or sad
about his family reunion. I had long-hoped that they would
find a way to reconcile, but at what cost?

Will they convince him that he should make our
separation permanent?
Would he actually leave me? Leave Janie?
Will they try to take her from me?

In two years she'll be an adult. How much poison could they pour into her in that amount of time?

No. Noah would never allow it.

Around five o'clock in the morning, the tide had shifted. The magnetic pull was again undeniable.

It was time to return to the boathouse. It was time to leave.

It was time to return to the actual bed that I had made for myself.

CHAPTER FIVE

FAITH

I had overslept. Rarely do I oversleep. But the sun was up and undeterred by the curtains in my room. I could hear my mother out in the kitchen chopping away on a cutting board. I looked over at the clock on my nightstand. It was shortly after ten. It made no sense.

I never sleep this late.

Then, I remembered being "out" late the night before.

Did it really happen? I must have been dreaming.

Scratching my head and yawning, I sat up in bed and looked around the room. Everything seemed normal, except for the amount of noise coming from the kitchen. I looked again at the clock to be sure I wasn't mistaken.

The sundial had been placed carefully on the nightstand beside the alarm clock. I dare not touch it.

Scooting out of bed, I slid my feet into my slippers and grabbed my robe from the hook behind the door.

"Good morning!" my mom called from the kitchen. She could hear me moving about. I wondered how long she would have been willing to let me sleep.

"Don't dilly-dally," she commanded. "We've got company coming in two hours!"

Oh, that's right. She invited Chrissy and Noah over for lunch. Ugh.

I sashayed my tired ass into the bathroom and went through my morning routine, including a hot shower. I stood beneath the showerhead for a long time, allowing the heat and steam to surround me, hoping it would help to clear my head. So much had happened in the past twenty-four hours: meeting Chrissy in the Acme, getting in the Jeep with Noah, Watching some guy named Nigel . . .

Wait . . . Nigel . . . he was preparing to jump . . . in both, what? . . . places?

It must have been a dream. It had to be a dream. It was all triggered by my subconscious. Right? I was probably thinking about Noah and the lighthouse incident when I fell asleep. That's got to be it.

But Janie, she's real. She's alive. It has to be. I held her. I talked with her . . .

My stomach was tying itself into knots. A lump was moving up my throat, so much so, I thought I would gag. It was difficult to swallow.

I stepped out of the shower and wrapped a towel around me. Pausing before the mirror, I studied my physical condition. (I already knew my mental state was whacked.)

Where have I been? What's happened to me? What about Janie?

Needing to anchor myself onto something solid and reliable, I grabbed hold of the vanity.

Who am I? Am I in the right place? What's real and what's not real?

"Faith, did you hear me?" my mother called from the kitchen.

OK, that's real . . .

My thoughts ran amuck in two different directions. I didn't know whether I should run back down to the boathouse and return to Janie, or stay put.

And what if I did return to Janie? I had two young children back in Seattle who needed me. Could I just disappear for two years until Janie became an adult? But... apparently, she's OK. She's been OK, and it seems I can't stay there.
The sundial.
What if I went back and then destroyed the sundial?

No! I can't stay there! I could never leave Charlie and Maddie... or Tyler.

And then it dawned on me: sitting on the nightstand, beside the alarm clock, was the one thing that connected both worlds together. Should anything happen to the sundial...
Then again, I could end it all by destroying the shell.

I gave up Janie once. Could I do it again?

"Faith! It's getting late. Are you OK in there?" Mom called again.
"Yes. I'm just moving slow this morning."
I began pulling a wide-tooth comb through my hair. It became tangled in a large, knotted mess behind my head.

This is something my conditioner should have taken care of.

I pulled harder. The comb was stuck. Things were going from bad to worse, so I yanked the comb free, laid it down on the vanity, and began working the snagged hair with my fingers. The knot was enormous.

What the hell?

I grabbed the hand mirror from the vanity and turned around to see the back of my head. The angle was just right to create the illusion of infinite mirrored reflections, except standing in the middle of one was a young lady with wide eyes and beautiful strawberry hair. The vision startled me.

The hand mirror fell from my hands and crashed to the floor, shattering everywhere.

"Faaaaaith!" my mother cried out, "What is going on in there?"

I looked down at my feet. The slivers of glass were still reflecting light, causing the floor to glisten like the sun's reflection on rippled water, just like the day Noah had rescued me.

"I'm fine, Mom. I dropped the mirror. I'll take care of it," I called back to the kitchen.

Stooping down to pick up the broken pieces, they immediately went to black when I touched them.

Studying the shards in a squat position, I became dizzy and feared that I might faint if I stood up too fast. I grabbed hold of the vanity, again, to steady myself.

"Mom," I called out warily, "come look at this."

Now I had reason to believe that something was out of order.

Would she see it too?

I heard her let out an annoyed huff as she put down her knife and made her way back to the bathroom.

"What is it?" she asked, wiping her hands on a tea towel, "I'm in the middle of making chicken salad."

"Look at the glass. I broke the mirror and the pieces are turning black when I pick them up. Is that normal?"

"Black? What are you talking about? Look at this mess! Be careful you don't step in any of it in your bare feet. There's likely to be tiny shards of glass all over the place. Now get it cleaned up. Use the vacuum so nothing is left behind."

"You don't see it? Look! This one is black!" I said as I dramatically held out a larger piece of the rounded rim.

"Stop playing around and get this disaster cleaned up!" Mom scolded. "Noah and Chrissy will be here in less than two hours. And for God's sake, be careful!"

"You don't see that?"

"See what?"

Clearly, something was wrong with me.

"Nothing . . . nothing. I'll get it cleaned up."

I swept up every tiny sliver, however, any shard that was large enough to hold in my hand, I carefully picked up and examined the phenomenon over and over again. Any time I touched the glass, it disappeared, as if the glass was absorbing all the light, rather than reflecting it back. I could feel it in my fingers, I just couldn't see it.

It's like looking into a black hole . . .
Jesus, what is happening to me?

Throughout the morning, I kept touching and picking up things. Mom caught my strange behavior and once again asked if I was OK.

Noah and Chrissy arrived right on time. Noah presented my mom with a bouquet of fresh cut flowers and Chrissy handed me a bottle of wine.

"It's chilled, so we can open it and have it with lunch!" Chrissy winked at me.

She makes it so difficult to dislike her. Deep inside, I knew I wanted a justifiable reason to hate her.

"So," Chrissy continued, "I understand you helped Noah talk Nigel down from the lighthouse gallery last evening."

"What?" My mom spun around, her mouth gaping open.

"Well, not really," I corrected. "Noah went up the lighthouse and talked Nigel down. I was on standby, for moral support, I suppose."

"Wait," Mom interrupted. "You were with Noah and someone climbed the lighthouse and then couldn't get down?"

"Not exactly," I started to explain.

Noah interceded.

"Nigel is a young man who is going through a difficult time right now . . . well, more like a difficult life, but we won't get into that. Anyway—and I would appreciate that none of this be discussed outside of this house out of respect for the young man—he was having a personal crisis and his mother called and asked me to come out to the lighthouse right away.

My mother looked back at me, confused, wondering why I was out with Noah in the first place. *This* I could read in her. Fortunately, she knew better than to hold an interrogation in front of Chrissy. Truth was, I also had no idea why Noah had taken me to the lighthouse.

NOAH

The luncheon had a bit of an awkward start, and then moved toward the bizarre. Much to my surprise, Chrissy and Faith were getting along just fine, at first. It could've had something to do with the wine, but probably had more to do with Chrissy's unique ability to connect with people she'd just met. No matter the age gap, gender, ethnicity, past crimes, and—as I had recently learned—their sexual orientation, Chrissy was able to empathize with them and expeditiously earn their trust. Faith was no exception to Chrissy's unique set of social skills.

Seated around Mrs. Cuthbertson's dining table that overlooked the North East River, Chrissy began in her usual way. She is very gifted in knowing how to uncover little known facts and stories about one's family, and life in general, without crossing into sensitive territories too soon. She had an impeccable sense of timing and pace. Like a bird of prey, she glides effortlessly on the thermals of small talk, lazily circling around casual conversation. Soothed by the comfort of her voice and the sincerity in her eyes, her prey drop their guard and submit. People happily share their worst nightmares and gravest moments with my wife. I should know. That's how she became intimately familiar with my past history with Faith. I remember how relieved I was to finally share my hurt with someone whom I considered safe and trustworthy with such information. (Only recently, since meeting Nigel, had she ever shared it with someone else.) At the time of my deepest confession, we were in the throes of discussing our future, and if we were to marry, she needed to hear it from me.

During lunch, Faith happily passed around photos of her two daughters, Charlie and Maddie. Her daughters looked like day and night, respectively. Charlie was very fair complexioned with beautiful blond curls. Her thick glasses gave away the possibility of physical and, perhaps, learning challenges. Maddie, on the other hand, had straight dark hair and a mischievous twinkle in her eyes.

Chrissy artfully waltzed her way into Faith's life.

"Charlie is absolutely beautiful. Was your hair that blond when you were her age?"

"Yes, that's probably where she gets it."

"I love the way she smiles at the camera with those big beautiful eyes!"

"Yes, she does have beautiful eyes, even her glasses can't take that away from her."

"How long has she been wearing glasses?"

"Oh, probably since she was three."

"That's young."

"Yes. That's' when we first became aware that she was having trouble. Her pre-school teacher, whom Charlie adored, noticed within days of her arrival that she was having trouble focusing on activities across the room, or playground, and suggested that we take her to a specialist."

"She's adjusted well, I presume?"

"Yes. We were quite worried at first, but she's going to be OK. She's really come a long way."

That was the opening Chrissy was looking for.

"A long way?"

"Yes, Charlie is a little different. She does have some learning disabilities. But she is the sweetest little girl you'd ever want to know," Faith said with glowing pride. "She delights in the smallest things that we would normally overlook or take for granted. She helps us to see and taste the world in a much more exquisite way."

"Yes, I imagine so. I can tell just by looking at her smile. I would love to meet her one day," Chrissy hummed.

"I'm sure that can be arranged!" Mrs. Cuthbertson jumped in. "Faith and Tyler and the girls come out to visit about once a year in July. You would just love them. We should have a little get together the next time they're here," Mrs. Cuthbertson suggested with great gusto.

"Mom," Faith demurred, "I'm sure Noah and Chrissy have a lot going . . ."

"No, no, we would love to meet your family!" Chrissy interrupted enthusiastically.

Faith looked at me for help. I could still read her signals; they hadn't changed in sixteen years. It was easy to see that she was uncomfortable with the sudden invitation offered up by her mother, completely disrupting the inroads Chrissy was making. I wiped my mouth with my napkin and laid it back down in my lap, realizing that everyone was waiting for me to add my two cents.

"We would love to meet your family, Faith."

"Well, they can be a handful," Faith explained as she brushed her fork through her untouched salad. "The girls don't sit still for very long."

"That's no problem," her mother assured her. "We could have a picnic on the dock. If the girls get bored, they could always take a swim while we talk."

"Mom, watching the girls while they're in the water is not relaxing, and certainly not conducive to holding a conversation," Faith countered. She turned and addressed Chrissy and me. "They—my girls—love to upset me by disappearing underwater, where I can't see them, and holding their breath as long as they can."

"Ornery, are they? Your girls get along well, it sounds," Chrissy prompted. "Sisters who play pranks together are usually very close."

"Very," Faith replied. "Hopefully, they'll remain that close when they reach puberty! They'll need each other. Though, sadly, I'm sure all bets will be off when they enter that stage in their lives."

"I hear that can be a rough time. Well, it wasn't exactly easy for me, now that I think back on it. Everything was wrong and it had to be someone else's fault. I blamed my parents for the most part," Chrissy shared humorously.

"Oh, Faith was a scamp," Mrs. Cuthbertson chortled as she rested her hand on Faith's arm. "Her older sister, Hope, was as easy as pie."

"Hope and Faith," Chrissy murmured, repeating their names.

"Yes, Abe and I didn't have the easiest time getting pregnant, thus their names. Now, Faith, on the other hand . . ."

"MOM!" Faith scolded, yanking her arm away from her mother's touch.

It rattled me too. For some reason, Faith easily became pregnant but was unable to carry our child. Her mother, it seemed, was about to bring it up in front of my wife. But alas, now Faith had two beautiful daughters of her own, something Chrissy and I will never have.

"I'm so happy for you, Faith," seemed like the right thing to say.

"Yes . . ." Chrissy solemnly agreed. "Noah and I, sadly, will never have children."

"No?" Faith asked quietly. "I'm so sorry."

"It's all right. We're learning to accept it. Aren't we, Noah?" Chrissy asked, placing her hand on mine. There was a lot of physical reaffirmation going on around the table, something Chrissy excelled at. Have you ever noticed how contagious that can be?

However, I hardly knew what to say. Chrissy's transparency was a lot to take in in recent days. There were secrets I would rather she had not shared with others. This was one of them. There are things that I would rather have remained between God and us. But in the past several weeks, Chrissy was without a filter, which was so uncharacteristic of her.

"Yes. I am sure God has other plans for us."

For the remainder of our time at the Cuthbertson residence, Faith seemed preoccupied, drifting in and out of our conversations—mostly out. It left Chrissy and me to converse mainly with Mrs. Cuthbertson who carried on about her granddaughters and her husband's passing, which made things uncomfortable and even heavy at times. Meanwhile, Faith was off in her own world. It was reminiscent of our breakup years ago.

FAITH

Have you ever had that moment when an idea pops into your head and you know you shouldn't act on it until you've thought it through? But, you act anyway. Then, afterward, you look back and realize that you should have taken the time to evaluate all of the possible outcomes, especially because you weren't real sure of the goal in the first place?

It happens to me more often than I care to admit. "Life is about choices," I seem to recall Mrs. McKenna repeating over and over again when she came to visit with my mother and me all those years ago, when she had learned that I was pregnant with Janie.

When Noah and Chrissy were preparing to leave, I followed Noah to the guest room where he had gone to retrieve Chrissy's jacket. I pretended I was going down the hall to use the bathroom. Out of sight, I grabbed Noah's arm. He spun around, shocked and confused. I guess I grabbed him a little more intensely than I had intended.

"I need to speak with you," I whispered.

Noah looked around to see if anyone was watching us. It must have been obvious to him that I was trying to be discreet in my request.

"Is everything OK with you?"

"Yes, yes. But there are a few things you need to know. I need to speak with you . . . alone."

"OK."

"Not now. There's not enough time. I need to meet with you privately."

"I don't know if that's such a good idea."

"Why not?"

"*This* doesn't feel right."

"What? You had no problem picking me up the other day. Why should this be any different? Trust me. I just need to talk to you about some unfinished business."

I had piqued Noah's curiosity. His eyes widened with speculation, trying to read into my request.

"Meet me tonight," I added.

"Tonight? That probably won't work. I have a meeting with the Elders at seven-thirty."

"Meet me at midnight, at the boathouse."

"Midnight? Here?"

"Yes. My mom will be asleep. No one will know."

"This sounds highly inappropriate."

"Don't be so self-righteous, and what do you take me for? It's just that there is something you need to know, and the sooner, the better. Plus, this is rather urgent, and sensitive. Please, Noah, trust me on this."

"And what do I tell Chrissy?"

"Nothing. She doesn't need to know, nor should she . . . at least not right away."

"I don't hide things from my wife, Faith," Noah snarled, yanking his arm from my grasp.

"If you want to know about your daughter—our daughter—you will be here, tonight."

Noah's eyes hardened.

"Pastor Noah! What's taking so long? Is everything OK?" my mom called from the front door where she was waiting with Chrissy.

"Everything's fine," Noah replied. His eyes never left mine, glaring at me as if I had just offended him in some way.

"Are you sure you're OK?" he asked again, scrutinizing my face for any signs of lunacy.

"You can trust me, Noah. And you need to hear what I have to say. Midnight. I'm not kidding."

The tide was due to begin flowing out at twelve-thirty AM. I had pretty much ascertained by then that in order to see Janie, I had to travel with earth's tidal rhythms. My successful visits only occurred with the outgoing tides.

Likewise, I would return with the incoming tides. Both times, the sundial had to be in my hands and I had to be peering into its illuminated concave spiral. Therefore, I would have to convince Noah to come along with me at a specific time. Hopefully, we could travel together.

That night, leaving nothing to chance, I walked down to the dock at eleven-thirty with the sundial in my hand. It was very dark. A heavy cloud cover was blocking any hope of a guiding light coming from the moon. So, I had to carefully make my way down the uneven terrain. The boathouse, its silhouette camouflaged by the night sky, was totally dark inside. No glow. No illuminations.

A fine layer of mist hung above the surface of the river, casting an eerie veil over its near and distant surroundings. The flashing channel markers were barely visible. Not a good time to be out on the water. Due to the lack of wind—not even an occasional breath of air—the river was like a sheet of glass and only hushed pulsations kissed the shoreline. All was quiet. No crickets or other night bugs. Not a peep from the water foul nestled in somewhere nearby. The sense of isolation was almost overwhelming.

I took a seat on one of the dew-covered dock chairs. A chill traveled up my spine, causing my body to shudder.

Thirty minutes and Noah should be here. How am I going to explain this to him? Will he even go for it? Or will he think I'm looney tunes and leave. I'll have to make him swear not to say a word to anyone, whether he believes my story or not. Whether he decides to go, or stay.

And if he elects not to go with me, or if the sundial won't take him with me, what happens? Do I just disappear before his eyes?

Time spent waiting for someone to arrive never passes quickly. That night was no exception. The high humidity dampened my clothes as I impatiently waited and waited and conjured up ways to explain all that had happened. I had to convince Noah of the possibility.

By one o'clock AM, my hopes were dashed by Noah's apparent no-show. It was approaching the time to give up. I turned to look back toward the driveway when I noticed a small glow in the boathouse that brightened as I approached the door.

Yes, It was time to go. I would have to go without him.

NOAH

I returned home from my meeting near ten-thirty. The late hour was highly unusual because I never allowed my Board of Elders to rehash an agenda item until it was beaten to death like a veal cutlet.

Chrissy knew something had gone wrong. The minute I came through the door she could tell that there was trouble.

"Your meeting ran late. Is everything OK?"

"Sit down, Chrissy. There's something I have to tell you."

Like an old married couple, I sat in my favorite chair, and Chrissy in hers.

"Nigel has asked to be baptized," I stated, keenly aware of how agitated I must have sounded.

"That's wonderful news! Aren't you excited?"

"I was, until the Elders—or should I say Harper, Carl Harper, put the kibosh on it."

"Why would he do that?"

"Because, as he said, 'Everyone knows that boy is a flaming fag.' "

"What? Did he really say that?"

"Yes."

"And what did *you* say?"

"Nothing. I waited to see if anyone else wanted to weigh in."

"And did they?"

"They sure did. We got into a big debate about whether or not a gay person can truly be a Christian."

"Oh, dear. How did that go?"

"How do you think it went? Harper is so opinionated and intimidating that no one dared to challenge him."

"Did you? Did you challenge him?"

"Yes. I had to. They were crucifying the young man, someone they don't even know."

"Good for you."

"Not really. Before the night was over, Harper lunged at me and said if I put Nigel in the baptistry, he would have my job."

"Can he do that?"

"Of course he can if he gets a majority of Elders to side with him."

Chrissy silently pondered the threat that I had received. When she had absorbed the full weight of it, she took a deep breath.

"Noah, you can't let that man bully you into submission. You, more than anyone, know God's greatest command: 'Love God with all our heart and love others as yourself.' You have to fight for Nigel. You have to educate your congregation and get them ready for this."

"There's no time for that. Nigel is ready now. He wants to be baptized now. Not in another year. But that means that I'll have to expose him to someone like Carl Harper. And that's how Nigel ended up on the lighthouse rail in the first place."

"You can't protect him from the realities of human nature. He has to learn to live in this world while leaning on God's promises. Noah? Are you even thinking of not allowing this baptism to take place?"

"Of course it will take place."

Aside from the mess going on at church, I also remembered Faith's invitation. I dared not share it with Chrissy, and I just couldn't accept Faith's invitation—or demand, I should say—for many reasons: the chief one being that my mind was pre-occupied with Nigel's request. Plus, it didn't feel right. She'd asked me to meet her near midnight and not tell my wife. The phrase "Don't tell your wife" is a red flag to any good marriage. I had never intentionally lied to Chrissy and I didn't plan on starting. As much as I wanted to know what "unfinished business" Faith thought I needed to hear, I didn't think conducting that conversation near the boathouse—our past, favorite rendezvous place—was appropriate. It's too close.

Sometimes, it's best to leave the past in the past, no matter what's been left undone.

FAITH

I returned the next morning before my mom was out of bed. Tip-toeing into my room, I placed the sundial on my dresser and removed my clothes.

How odd, just minutes ago, I was in this very room, watching Janie sleep.
I must be losing my mind.
I need to talk to someone.

I needed to talk to Noah. If I tried to explain this to Mom, she would think I was nuts. And Tyler . . .

How could I even begin to explain this to my family?

Noah was my only option. Noah needed to know. He needed to know that he had . . . *or has* . . . a daughter.

I reflected back on having lunch with him and Chrissy just the day before. Hearing that they would never have children was . . . well, I don't quite know how to say it without sounding like I'm gloating. Their inability to have children meant that I would be the only one. Janie would be Noah's only legacy. I had something of Noah's that Chrissy could never give him.

If I could just get him to go with me.

Was I relieved? Was I that heartless that I would actually gloat about this?

Am I that person?

Sleep. I needed sleep. I had been up most of the night, and now I was feeling sick and half delirious. I crawled into bed and under the covers. Plus, I did not like what I was seeing in myself.

As I drifted off, I prayed that my mother would not disturb me when she woke up.

Hours later, I started to stir. I lay in bed half awake, imagining Charlie and Maddie tucked into their beds back in Seattle. Charlie's blond hair would be just peeking out from under the covers into which she would have cocooned herself. Her glasses would be nearby on the nightstand. Maddie, the antithesis of her older sister, would be sprawled out in some undetermined direction. She tended to move around a lot in her sleep. Lord only knew in what position we would find her in the morning. Her pillow was most likely kicked to the floor with all her blankets pooled on either side of the bed, yet her stuffed rabbit would be within reach. Asleep or awake, that girl was never still.

Tyler, my dear husband, would be lying on his left side, facing the empty hollow left by my absence in our king bed. More than likely, his right arm was thrust out, as if I were there. He was probably snoring: a sound that I now missed. I wanted to go home. I missed my family. I especially missed my girls. In a few hours, they would be waking up to another morning without me. I had been gone almost a week. I felt so disconnected. The haunting of my past was now pushing me beyond the familiar and preoccupying my every thought.

And then it struck me:

What will happen to Janie when I return to Seattle?

I had to tell Noah. He had to know. He could continue visiting with Janie after I was gone and then he could let me know how she was doing.

What is wrong with me? This can't be. And if it's remotely possible, how could I leave her again? She's only sixteen.

I must be going crazy. This isn't possible.

I'm losing it . . .

I've got to get out of this room.

The house was silent. I looked over at the clock on my nightstand. It was almost ten o'clock. The sun was up. I could hear an outboard motorboat bouncing down the river. (Outboard engines have a very distinct sound.) That meant that either a good breeze was churning up the river, or there was a lot of boat traffic, which would be unusual for a weekday.

I have to get out of bed and find Noah.

My mother had left a note for me on the kitchen counter:
"Off to the Acme."
Great. She drove herself, which she shouldn't have done, and now I'm stuck here without a car.

My mother had a wall phone with an extra long cord, the kind that twirled around itself and knotted up. As I lifted the receiver from the hook, I remembered spending long hours tucked around the corner and halfway down the hall, talking to Noah and running up his long distance phone charges. He, or his parents, didn't seem to mind, at the time.
My mother had the church office number on speed dial. Hopefully, Noah would be in his office.
Noah's phone began ringing and I waited. And waited. Just when I was about to give up, an out of breath Pastor Noah McKenna answered.
"Hello? Pastor Noah speaking."

I remember that husky breathlessness . . .

"Noah? It's Faith. I need to see you. Right away."
"Listen, about last night . . ."

CHAPTER SIX

FAITH

"I didn't 'survive,' Noah. Something's wrong. I think I might be having a nervous breakdown, or something. I think I saw our daughter."

"What? What are you talking about?"

"I saw our daughter."

Noah didn't respond. The line went silent.

"Noah, are you there?"

"I'm here . . ."

"I have to see you. We need to talk. You're the only one I can talk to about this."

"You said 'daughter.' You said 'daughter?' "

"Yes, Noah. We had a girl. Her name is Janie."

"You named the baby?"

"Yes, Noah. Her name is Janie, and she looks just like you."

"I'm so sorry, Faith," Noah murmured into the receiver. "Were you dreaming?" he tried to reason. He sounded confused, yet trying to remain sympathetic. Of course he was confused.

"No. I wasn't a dreaming. At least I don't thing I was. I don't understand what's happening, or how it's possible, but I'm telling you I saw our daughter. More than once. She's here, Noah . . . or there . . . wherever. The boathouse, it starts in the boathouse. She's here, but she's not here, here."

"Faith. You must have been dreaming. Medications. Are you taking any medications that might cause these dreams or hallucinations, maybe? Under a lot of pressure or stress?"

"No . . . I'm telling you that I have been with our daughter. It's definitely not a dream."

"Faith . . . wait. What are you saying?"

"I'm saying I have been with Janie . . . our daughter. She's sixteen, now."

"Faith . . ." Noah purred with his ultra soothing voice, exuding the same compassion I recalled from years long gone.

"Noah, I'm telling you. I've seen our daughter. I've been with her."

"Faith, you lost the baby. Remember?"

"Not exactly. That's why I couldn't see you before you left for college."

"What?"

"She's alive, Noah. You have a daughter!"

"Wait. So, you're saying that you *didn't* lose the baby? Faith . . ."

"Noah . . . there's something I need to tell you."

"You had the baby? Did you . . .? Did you give her up?" Noah whispered, fearful of the answer.

"No."

"But you said she's here."

"Not exactly here . . . now."

"Then what are you saying?"

"Noah, I'm saying we had a baby girl."

"So you had the baby? So everything about losing the baby was a ruse?"

"Not exactly."

"You lied to me? You lied to me about . . . my own child?"

Noah's voice was now turning hostile; all sympathy was fading away, which I could understand. I had handled the conversation all wrong. Left to draw his own conclusion, Noah was growing angrier with each word.

"I prefer not to talk about this on the phone. If you want to know what happened, we need to talk face-to-face. Just you and me, and I will tell you everything. At least as much as I can understand."

Fearing further escalation, I became desperate. Noah could choose to refuse any further communication with me if I didn't get this straightened out.

NOAH

Usually, I am a very patient man. I have the ability to separate myself from a given situation—compartmentalize, as my colleagues like to call it—and act with rational discretion. That has never been the case with Faith. From the first time I'd met her, I've never had a rational thought when I was around her. That, in and of itself, explains how she became pregnant. I'm not denying my responsibility. It's just recognizing and admitting my weakness when Faith was—or is—involved.

That frantic phone call was no different, except that Faith was making no sense at all, unless, of course, she had lied to me years ago about losing the baby. In which case, I should have been furious and justifiably so. No matter, I had to see her as requested.

When I arrived at the Cuthbertson residence, I noted that her mother's car was gone, which meant that we would be alone. As a pastor, this is a bit concerning. In seminary, we are cautioned about meeting with members of the opposite sex without a witness, or making sure we were in a very public place. This scenario met neither criterion.

As Faith had instructed, she was waiting down on the dock. She must have heard my Jeep coming down the sandy gravel lane. When I parked and hopped out, she stood and waved. It was a scene all too familiar.

Admittedly, she looked lovely. As a married man and a pastor, I knew better than to have those thoughts, but it was the truth. The past sixteen years had served her well. No longer was she the young girl that I had fallen in love with years ago. She was a mature woman, now, who managed to keep her bright smile and the effervescent sparkle of her youth in her eyes. Though still very active and fit, her body had gained some new curves over the years, adding an attractive mystique to her appearance.

And even though she sounded distraught on the phone, her countenance was belying it.

Yes, Faith would somehow always manage to be alluring to me. And, Chrissy was right: I sin every day. I am a pastor, but I am very much a carnal man.

Fortunately, Faith did not run up the dock to greet me as she would have done in the past. If she had, I am sure I would have caught her in my arms like old times. It felt as though not a day had passed since the last time . . .

Isn't this why I moved here? Isn't this what I had always hoped for? Why . . .? Why, now, do I have to see her alone? If this reunion had happened years ago . . .

So much has changed between us, making this a bad idea. I shouldn't be here. Nothing good can come from this.

As I walked toward her to say hello, Faith held out her arms and leaned into me. It was as natural as gathering up a lost puppy. A tender cuddle. A needed reassurance that I was there and everything was going to be OK. But as I held her, old feelings returned. The way her body fit into mine; her new body, softer and full of remembrance. The touch of her head upon my shoulder. The way she gently stroked my back as she held me. In that moment, I recollected and cherished all of the customary things we had shared. She even smelled the same, which was disconcerting because it had always brought forth an arousal in me. That day, I sadly admit, was no different.

I gently pushed her back, dislodging our bodies.

"You said you needed to see me."

"Please, Noah, you should sit down."

I pulled out a chair from the table, indicating that she should sit first, thinking she would accept my chivalrous offer. But, no. Faith demanded that I sit in the chair while she remained standing. Then, she paced about as she stammered through her story.

I listened in complete disbelief. Well, to be frank, I wanted to disbelieve what she was telling me because it meant that my mother, and her mother, and she had conspired and agreed to lie to me. When asked, she even confessed that her father knew, which explained why he always seemed to be in so much pain, and eventually, even sympathetic toward me.

Faith had had an abortion. She had aborted our child. My only chance to have children.

"STOP! Just stop! You're telling me that you didn't 'lose' the baby. The baby was perfectly fine when your mother took you to New York? And you did this without telling me? Without consulting me?"

"Yes . . . I'm so sorry, Noah," Faith whimpered as she reached out toward me.

I jumped out of my chair and backed away.

"Oh, that's so easy for you to say now, isn't it?"

"No. No it isn't. I wanted the baby as much as you did. It's just that our mothers convinced me it would be best for both of us if I had an abortion and not tell you. It all sounds so stupid, now."

"Stupid? Stupid isn't the word for it!"

"Your mother said it would 'kill you to know, and that you should go on to college with a clear head.' Those were her exact words. I remember them because that's what I kept telling myself, even as they were putting me under. I loved you, Noah. I thought it would be best. I wanted what was best for you, for us. I was seventeen."

"How could you know what was best for me? We had options, Faith. I told you I would go through hell and high water for you, and the baby. Wasn't that enough? Couldn't you hold on to *my* words, Faith? Couldn't you believe in me?"

"We were just kids. I was scared."

"And I suppose you figured an abortion was best for our baby?"

Faith burst into tears.

"I would have loved her, too, Noah. I didn't want to do it. I wanted you. I wanted all of it, but at what cost? We were so young and I was convinced that having a baby would be throwing everything away."

"Do you hear yourself? So you threw the baby away instead," I said with ugly, accusatory resignation.

Faith collapsed in a chair, deliberately avoiding eye contact with me. She had disappeared somewhere into the depths of her remorse, into the memory of what she had done.

I remained standing off, with no desire to be near her. She had betrayed me. She took the life of my child without an ounce of consideration. Perhaps this was my punishment: knowing what had really happened. And to top it off, the people I loved the most had lied to me.

"Noah . . ." Faith whispered. "I can take you to see her."

"What? Her grave?"

"No. I mean I can take you to see *her*. She's sixteen and beautiful. She adores you and admires you."

"You're nuts. What's happened to you, Faith?"

"I'm serious, Noah. I can take you to see her. She's as alive as you are standing here on this dock. I can take you to her."

"Faith, there's no need to try to placate me by making things up. This is so over the line. What's done is done. No more lies. No more of whatever this is."

I had heard enough and turned to leave.

"NO! Wait!" Faith implored. "I can take you to see her."

Faith reached into her pocket and brought forth a shell that I immediately recognized.

FAITH

"Do you remember this shell?" I asked hurriedly, afraid he was going to walk away.

Noah stared at my hand.

"Yes."

"You said it would bring me comfort and healing."

"I know what I said," Noah stated abrasively.

"It can take us to her.

"Faith . . ." Noah whispered, almost sympathetically. "That's a myth. Something to make you *think* you can find comfort and healing. It's symbolic. It has no actual power".

"Noah, I'm telling you, I can take you to her."

I stood, and with renewed courage I explained how the out-going tide would carry me if I stood in the boathouse, on the exact same spot where Janie was conceived. I described what would happen when all conditions were met and the light coming through the floorboards illuminated the shell. I swore that if my eyes followed the concave spiral into the shell, I could visit with Janie.

OK. Now that I've said it out loud, it does sound ridiculously contrived.

"Trust me, Noah. Please. Just this once. If we don't succeed, I won't speak of it again."

Noah glared at me, evaluating the insanity of my whacked-out proposal.

A strong wind suddenly blew through the trees and the tide began racing out. The leaves blown to the water's surface were being swept away by the accelerating current. The river was becoming agitated and a fast-moving chop was rapidly churning into something more serious.

"Please, Noah. I can take you . . . now. We need to go into the boathouse. Let's go. Now."

I had to strike while the iron was hot. If he left, I knew he would never return and any hope of introducing him to his daughter would be lost. There would be no one to look after Janie once I returned to Seattle.

"We can't go into the boathouse. I can't go into the boathouse alone with you."

"Don't be afraid, Noah. Trust me. You have to trust me. You have a daughter, Noah. Don't you want to meet her?"

Noah backed away.

I was being too forceful. I was losing him. The wind continued to intensify. In order to be heard over the acceleration of all the forces surrounding us, Noah raised his voice.

"This is nuts, Faith. You know that."

"It's not. If you don't want to go into the boathouse with me, then go alone."

"You're on the verge of . . . heresy . . . to believe in any power other than the power of God is heresy, Faith. You can't do this. I won't do this."

"How do you know this is not of God? You always say 'His ways are not our ways.' I'm telling you the truth, and anything true is of God. You preached it yourself," I shouted back at him.

"But God would not have wanted you to abort the baby in the first place," Noah countered, all-knowingly.

I was at a loss for words. I had to acknowledge his claim in order to get him to see beyond the soapbox from which he preached every Sunday. I had to get him out of his narrow comfort zone.

"True. But he is a God of second chances, isn't he? Despite the choices we've made . . . that I've made . . . He gives us a second, third, a fourth, infinite chances. Isn't that what you tell everyone?"

The wind was beginning to howl around the corner of the boathouse. Noah raised his voice another notch.

"What is it you want me to do, Faith? Stand in the boathouse and stare into the shell as you described? Is that it, and then you will let this go?"

"Yes."

I was silently praying amidst the rage that Noah would do just that.

"All right, then. Give me the shell."

I glanced over at the boathouse window and sure enough, the glow had returned and was intensifying. Noah saw it too.

"This is insane. You've lost your mind. But if this will put an end to it . . ." he said as he grabbed the shell from my hand. "I can't believe you saved this thing after all these years," I faintly heard him mutter.

Noah staggered against the wind to the door and pulled it open, scraping it along the dock.

"Do I have to pull this door closed behind me? It's going to come off its hinges."

"No. I've always left it open. Just go to the center of the floor, hold the shell over the light and stare into the concave spiral and let your eyes follow it . . . no matter what happens, stay with it."

Noah smirked, just as he used to whenever I suggested something silly or juvenile to amuse him. Then he muttered something inaudible as he entered the boathouse.

The wind was whipping across the river creating a dense multitude of dark whitecaps. A solitary sailboat was in the channel, its bow slamming into each cresting wave as someone onboard was battling before the mast, trying to lower the mainsail. The sail was luffing wildly as the captain at the helm tried to hold the boat into the wind. The gale howled and shoved everything in its path. The old boathouse creaked and shuddered as if it would be blown off the dock. A few seconds later, above all of the noise and chaos, I heard Noah calling my name. He was frantic.

"Faith! FAITH!"

I ran in to him. His eyes were rolling up in his head as he remained standing in the middle of the floor with an arm out stretched. Without a second thought, I grabbed his hand and instantly felt as if I would throw up.

And then it stopped, as though someone had slammed on the brakes and sent me flying forward without a seatbelt. Except, I didn't hit the dashboard. I was in Noah's arms.

"Faith, don't let go. Don't give up on us. Come back home. I know we can make this work."

Noah and I were standing in the boathouse. He had found me there, hanging up the wet lifejackets Janie and I had just taken off. She and I had been out on the dinghy. Now, Janie was in a hurry to return to the house, running past her father, stopping only long enough to hug him and say, "Hello, Daddy!"

Darla was on her way over and would soon arrive.

Noah, as handsome and humble as ever, began his pleading.

"I miss you and Janie. I even miss that stupid dog."

So much had passed between us, good and bad. We knew each other so well, it was on the brink of annoying. Yet, apart from each other, we were irrefutably unhappy. Love him, or hate him, Noah was a part of me. And the truth was: I had never stopped loving him, even in his worse moments . . . or mine, for that matter. Even through the most hellish of times, I had never stopped loving Noah McKenna. I would always love him. Always.

"What about your family? I'm sure a reconciliation between us is not going to make them happy."

"They only want what's best for me, and Janie."

"Janie? They don't even know her."

"If they want me, they will have to take all of us. All three of us. Otherwise, they never had me in the first place."

"You make it sound so easy."

"No. It's never easy. But it's just that simple."

"Simple, huh? What about the drinking, Noah? What about the late nights at the bar and the little hussy you've been meeting there?"

Noah's face fell. He was caught, and embarrassed, and even ashamed, as well he should have been.

"Nothing happened, Faith. Nothing. She's just a professor from the Community College going through a rough patch."

"Sure."

"She was just looking for an ear. Someone to listen. She's new to the area. No family, no friends."

"And you believed her? You're so naïve. Even if it were true, the fact remains that you've sought solace and confided in someone other than me. How do you think that makes me feel? I'm just supposed to go on as if nothing happened?"

"Nothing happened, I'm telling you. It was just a few drinks and . . . conversation."

"Conversation. You were sharing 'conversation.' We all know what conversation leads to. Where did *she* think it was headed? It would have been one thing if you had only met up once by sheer chance, but you kept going back. Hear my words: You kept going back to her."

"No . . . she kept finding me. I never went looking for her."

"I'm supposed to believe that? Meanwhile, Janie and I were here. Waiting. Hoping. Getting used to new routines that didn't include you. And now, you expect us to pick up and do it all over again because you're ready to be a husband and a father? What about us? What about what we've been through?"

"I'm sorry. But if my memory serves me right, you're the one who left me. You. Left. Me. You took Janie and left a note. A scribbled note, Faith. You left me a goddamn note. Tell me that wouldn't drive you to drink or perhaps look for solace, which I didn't, by the way."

"I can't even believe you are trying to justify yourself."

"And how do you justify your actions? Huh? Tell me that. You took Janie from me . . ."

"I left thinking that some space would help us. That we would be able to see clearer. But apparently, you're in a rush to move on," I challenged.

Noah raised his hand. I thought he was going to strike me. The usually calm and coolheaded Noah was instinctively going to hit me for what I had just accused him of doing.

"Don't ever say that again!" he leaned in toward me, thrusting his finger in my face. "I would die for you. I would probably kill for you. I have been completely captivated and insane for you since the first time I saw you. There is nothing I wouldn't do for you . . . or Janie."

And then he broke down. It was the first time I had ever seen him cry. He fell to his knees as his heart broke and shattered into a million pieces beneath his heaving chest. It was a sight I could not bear, not for one second. I immediately dropped down beside him and took his head into my hands and drew him into my breasts, as a mother would do with a wounded child.

"Please, Noah. Don't cry. Please don't cry. This has been hard on all of us."

Noah's arms reached around me as we collapsed farther into each other, sitting in a homologous heap on the floor, the same floor where Noah and I had always sought privacy and shared our most intimate moments, where Janie had ultimately been conceived.

How I needed this man. We would find a way to make it work. It wasn't like we could erase the weeks that had passed, weeks spent separated. But the truth was, I couldn't go on without him and he had just assured me that he had learned the same.

In each other's arms—dare we let go again—we talked about our need to pull our family back together. Noah even joked about welcoming "that stupid dog" back into his life. (Actually, Noah loved Jed as much as Janie did, which is why he mocked the poor thing so much.)

Our biggest concern was how to present all of this to Janie. It would be another upheaval at the age of sixteen, though we knew she would eagerly welcome the chance for us to be reunited as a family.

"Best to do it quickly. Tell her it was all a big mistake," Noah suggested.

"Tell her that my choice to leave was a big mistake? I'm not sure that is the message I want to send her. Why not tell her the truth: that we were having issues and needed some space to figure it out. That no matter what, we never stopped fighting for our marriage . . . for our family. That was the real fight, and one worth having. Tell her that you missed her . . . and her stupid dog," I laughed.

"I guess you're right. She needs to learn to be a fighter, not a quitter."

"Right. We never quit. Do we? Even when you're in the bar, late at night," I stated with laser-sharp sarcasm.

Quite frankly, I knew his choice of "escape" was innocent, yet it would hang over us like a dark cloud, only because I would never let it go. Noah would be making up for that for a long time. I think he knew it, too.

Noah and I walked back up to the house to find that Darla had already picked up Janie. Just as well, it was definitely not the time to tell Janie that we would be moving back home, and hopefully the next day.

"Spend the day with me," Noah asked as soon as he realized we were alone. "Spend the day and the night, and every night hereafter."

Noah took my hand, and pulled me in close.

"I think a little lovemaking is just what the doctor would prescribe for us. I've been deprived far too long. It's not healthy. I'm wasting away here," Noah simpered as he looked down below his waist.

"I doubt that."

Noah took my hand and drew it to the crotch of his jeans. My fingers instinctively tightened around the bulge beneath his denim, undeniably enjoying the hardened effects of my touch.

"Ah, Faith," Noah moaned as he set his lips upon mine. Were he not my husband of almost seventeen years, I don't know how I would have reacted. But right then, all I could do was melt into his lips and around his searching tongue. With exquisite intensity, yet gentle stroking, Noah had dissolved every concern I had had and left me begging that he would carry me off to bed before anyone returned home.

NOAH

I woke up in a panic.

Where am I? What happened?
What am I doing in bed . . . and naked?

I quickly looked to the other side of the bed. Chrissy had left for her classes at the community college hours ago.

But I distinctly remember being with Faith . . . and I had met a beautiful young lady named Janie.
Was it possible? Everything . . . all of it . . . seemed so real. Did I really have a daughter? Do I have a daughter?

"No! WAIT!" I cried out clearly recalling that I had made love to Faith.

It felt real. It still feels real.

It *was* real. It had happened. There was no doubt.
I carefully slipped out from the sheets entangling me and jumped into the shower. They say that muscles have memory; that if you practice a routine over and over again, your muscles will remember and eventually take over. As I stood beneath the hot water, that muscle, if you will, clearly remembered. As I recalled the feel of her exploding around me, I remembered all of it. I was guilty as hell. Worse yet, I had delighted in it. I had detonated within her. Standing in the shower, I was aroused just thinking about it.

If you are reading this, and hate me now for what happened, I can certainly understand. I hated myself for what I had done. But here's the thing, I wasn't here. I was *there*. And I was married *there* . . . I was married to Faith. And the bigger, more important part of the whole event: I had a daughter. Out *there*, somewhere, I had a sixteen-year-old child and my only way to her was through Faith.

My God, I have a daughter...

In a pair of briefs and a robe, I went out to the living room and sat in my favorite chair and prayed. In my shame for my actions, and my joy for having met my daughter, there was no one else to turn to other than the One who is greater than I. One who knows the truth. One who is the Truth.

My prayers had offered no answers. That was not a surprise to me. Just as I had preached many times from the pulpit, God does not always answer our prayers in our time, and we must learn patience and trust. That all things will work for good.

Will they? Do they? Really?

Don't judge me. Even pastors have their doubts, at times.

So many questions were now turning toward the present. Do I tell Chrissy about what had happened? All of it, or just the part of it... about Janie? No. First, she would never believe it. No one in their right mind would believe the journey that I had taken. Then Chrissy would probably rationalize that I was just imagining it, or dreaming it, because deep down I could not bear that she and I would never have children.

If she could ever imagine or believe it, it would devastate her. Knowing now that I have, or had, a daughter would change the steadfast promises we had made to one another, including "no secrets." She would have every right to feel as though I had betrayed and misled her. Lied to her. When in fact, I had had no idea.

So, now, I would have to keep this a secret. A secret that belonged to Faith and me.

And what about Janie? I remembered what it felt like being *"there,"* being so excited that I would be moving back home and that the three of us were going to be a family again. The pain and waiting were finally over. Faith and Janie, and even Jed, were coming back home.

Why is it that I remember everything so clearly, yet while I was "there," I had no recollection of "this" reality? Of Chrissy? Of being a pastor?

I doubled back and began questioning everything again.

That's it. It wasn't real. It can't be real.
I will prove it to myself. I will go back to Faith and demand that she take me "there" again. She'll laugh at me, because it wasn't real. But it wasn't a dream either. Maybe it was closer to a near-death experience?
So, I had seen the dead?
NO! NO! Janie is NOT dead! She is as real as real can be.
I saw her. I touched her. I held her in a father-daughter embrace. She called me "Daddy." I can still hear her voice. I even have memories of her childhood. I know as much as a father can know about their sixteen-year-old daughter. I have to go back.

Confusion and strong doubts are a bad combination.

It was the phone ringing that eventually shook me from a state of near hysteria. I staggered out to the kitchen, rubbing my eyes, and took the receiver off the hook just in time to pick up the call. It was Nigel. I was late for our meeting.

"Hello?"

"Hello, Pastor Noah? It's Nigel. Weren't we supposed to meet today?"

"Yes, I'm sorry, I forgot to set my alarm and . . ."

It was well past noon. I sounded ridiculous, about to state that I had overslept.

"I'm sorry, Nigel. Can you meet me at my house? I can put together some sandwiches here and we can talk. Would that be OK?"

"Sure, Pastor. I'll be right over."

"Take your time."

My gears shifted into pastor mode as I got dressed and mentally reviewed what it was I needed to discuss with Nigel. In my rushing about, I prayed that God would show me exactly how to bring Nigel into the fold. How I could best counsel him and guide him forward in the path that he should go. *(I know, pastor-speak . . .)* Honestly, though, I was such a wreck, I didn't know which direction was up. Being distracted by Nigel's visit would be good for me.

I prayed, and even cursed, as I got ready for the day ahead.

Having already spoken with Mrs. Cuthbertson about the possibility, it was my plan to baptize Nigel in the North East River, in front of the Cuthbertson residence. Mrs. Cuthbertson readily accepted my proposal and was excited to help. She even volunteered to host a small luncheon after the ceremony for Nigel's family and his good friend Emily. I had cautioned Mrs. Cuthbertson that Nigel's possible baptism was raising the hackles of some of the church elders and would probably prick the ire of many church members, too. Therefore, I thought it might be best to do everything quietly.

"Why?" she had asked. "Why should this young man receive anything less than anyone else? Because he's gay? Shame on all of us if we have to think twice about celebrating a young man's baptism."

"Mrs. Cuthbertson, I happen to agree with you. But I have to let you know that I have received threats regarding the possibility of baptizing Nigel in the baptistry. That's why I'm here. But I am concerned for your safety if we make this into a big deal."

"The bigger, the better! This *is* a big deal! Every baptism is a big deal."

And that's why I had asked Nigel to meet with me. We were going to talk in more depth about what it means to "go down to the river."

Nigel had agreed to all of the arrangements. His mother agreed. Chrissy thought it would be a beautiful event in an authentic setting; that Nigel should be so blessed. Emily was excited to attend. His maternal grandparents were making the trip from Richmond.

In the midst of all this, I had Sunday's sermon to finish and rehearse. The baptism would take place on Saturday. And to be transparent, I would proclaim on Sunday what had taken place the day before.

My nerves were shot. How was I going to present this?

"Whenever you are arrested or brought to trial, do not worry beforehand about what to say. Just say whatever is given to you at the time, for it is not you speaking, but the Holy Spirit." Mark 13:11

This announcement was sure to split the congregation in two.

FAITH

It was the afternoon of the next day when I heard a car coasting down the lane. It was Noah's Jeep.

"Oh, what a surprise!" my mother said. "Noah's here. Were you expecting him?"

"No . . ." I responded.

"He must be here to discuss that young man's baptism tomorrow. Poor Noah, so much stress. I don't know why those elders don't just let him do his job," Mom lamented.

"Who's being baptized?"

"Nigel. The young man Noah pulled down from the lighthouse."

"He didn't *pull* him down, Mom. No one was pulled down. Nigel came down because he was ready to."

"No matter. It's all semantics. The point is: Nigel is going to become a Christian!"

"Uh . . . I think he *is* a Christian, Mom. He just wants to make it official."

"Oh, Faith. You should go to church. And you need to get the girls into Sunday school. How are they, by the way?"

"Can we not get into it? The girls and Tyler are fine."

And now my stomach's in knots and Noah is walking toward the door.

I loved Tyler. I loved my family. I loved my life in Seattle. But the other truth was that now I knew and loved Janie, too.

And what about Noah? What about what had happened the day before? Am I responsible for that? Had I committed another one of the "Thou Shalt Nots?"

I remembered Noah saying—in the one and only service of his that I had attended, other than my father's funeral—that "whatever is true, is of God. God *is* Truth."

Noah politely knocked on the door, shaking me from my philosophical thoughts and self-sanctifying rationalizations.

"Hi, Noah. Were we expecting you?" I asked cautiously.

"No. I just happened to be in the area and thought I'd stop by. Do you have a couple minutes?"

"Sure."

"Let's go down to the dock where we can talk?" he whispered, peering around my shoulder to indicate my mother's listening ears and insatiable curiosity concerning all things "Pastor Noah McKenna."

Can someone explain peoples' fascination with pastors' lives?

"Sure. We'll be back, Mom."

"Everything set for tomorrow, Pastor?" my mom asked in some weird cajoling way.

"Yes, Mrs. Cuthbertson. Just some logistical things I need to discuss with Faith. Would you excuse us, please?"

"Of course," my mom replied with a raised eyebrow.

Noah and I made our way down the gentle, rutty slope to the dock. It felt like old times—Noah walking close beside me—except he wasn't holding my hand.

In short order, we were standing on the dock, above the water.

"Yesterday," he started, "it really happened?"

"Yes."

Noah turned to me with a hand raised to his forehead, rubbing it in confusion and distress.

"I have a daughter . . . Janie?"

"Yes."

His mood turned. He was angry. Angrier than I had ever seen him before.

"How long have you known this? How long have you been hiding her from me? And how long have you been visiting her? And who the hell is raising her?"

Noah swore. He used to swear all the time when we were dating. But this really took me by surprise.

"I just learned . . . I mean I just met her this week. It just happened this week, for the first time. I visited with her exactly three times before taking you to her. And for your information, *we* are raising her, apparently."

"That's impossible."

"Is it? Then why is it that we know everything about her? Remember her first birthday when we let her dive into her cake? Remember when she would only wear that T-shirt with the sparkly little pony on it? Remember when she brought Jed home from the baseball field and at first you said she couldn't keep him?"

"Stop! Yes, I remember all those things . . . and more."

"Remember the note I left when I took Janie and Jed and went back to my mother's?"

"Yes. It was mean and cowardly."

"And, you remember yesterday . . ."

"Stop."

"No, I won't stop. I won't stop because I am living with this too. And it's killing me, as well. Janie and I were due to return home today . . . to return back to you. Do you remember that?"

"Faith . . . This can't be."

Noah—like me—was struggling with the whole concept of what was happening, or could have happened, whatever it was that we had been through in yesterday's journey. He turned away from me, placing his hands on his narrow hips. He threw his head back and faced up toward the sky as if he were talking to God.

"Noah?" I whispered after an appropriate amount of time. "The tide is running out. We should go."

"Go?" he asked tersely as he spun back around. "Go where? Back to us?"

"Back to Janie. I have to return to Seattle next week, and I need you to look in on her from time to time while I'm gone."

"No. I can't do that. I can't do *this*. I can't start lying to Chrissy and I certainly can't tell her. I'm all she has. I just can't do this."

"And what about Janie? What is it you won't do for her?"

NOAH

"For her? I don't even . . ."

"Know her? You were going to say that you don't even know her. That's what you were going to say. Isn't it? But, you *do* know her. You know her, probably better than most fathers know their daughters. You've been teaching her how to drive. You showed her how to change a tire. You've been to all of her softball games. You put up with her violin lessons," Faith recalled accurately.

I even caught myself laughing at the mention of that awful violin. Jed would howl and I'm pretty sure the neighbors were cringing. Poor Jed, we eventually had to shut him in our room whenever Janie practiced. Fortunately, she dropped violin and stuck with softball in high school. She was a darn good shortstop.

It was all true. Standing there with Faith, I could not deny any of it, and I *was* missing Janie. I was missing her deeply and wanted to be with her again in a way I had never known before. My heart was aching to see my "little girl" again.

"If we're going to go, we have to go now," Faith warned.

"This is so wrong on so many levels. This can't be of God. This can't be . . ."

"Oh stop with the God stuff. You make it sound like he's only as big as your imagination."

"You stop!"

"No, I won't. And Janie is not your imagination. She's real. That we know. We had a daughter. That much is true. And we, for whatever reason, have been given a way to see her. True? Yes. We should go."

Faith was in such a hurry.

"Please, Noah. We're wasting time"

"Doggone it! Why do I always have to give in to you?"

"And thank goodness you do, otherwise we wouldn't have Janie," Faith stated wryly.

Faith always knew how to push my buttons. I didn't know whether to be furious or grateful. No matter, the pull was undeniable. I had to go.

We entered the boathouse and I took Faith's hand. She wrapped her fingers around mine and smiled.

"Hold tight, Noah. The tide is running fast. Don't let go."

Faith raised the sundial. The light coming through the old floorboards illuminated the coils within the shell, drawing me into its illusory staircase. My chest collapsed. My mental faculty dislodged from my physical body. I was in so much pain, but I held on tight to Faith's hand, which now felt like skin and bones. I knew she was there even though I couldn't see her in our hyper-spin. I remember shouting out to God, and Faith screaming in distress.

When the rush of oxygen reentered my lungs, it hurt just as much as when all the air had left me. I turned and looked at Faith.

She was calm and radiant. She had become the best thing I had seen in days. And she was with me. We were standing at our front door.

"Welcome home, Faith."

"Its good to be here."

"Please, don't ever do that again. Don't ever leave me."

"I'm so sorry, Noah. I wish we could get back to what we once had. I really miss that."

"I do, too."

"Only this time it will be better, because we know—now—how bad it can be without each other."

"I feel the same," I eagerly confessed as I drew her close to me and exhaled. Being with Faith was as natural as breathing. Holding her close was like wrapping up in a favorite blanket in front of a cozy fire. Faith was oxygen to me. She was my life.

"Mmmm . . ." she hummed into my chest. "Our luggage is in the car."

"It can wait."

"I have to pick up Janie from softball practice in forty minutes."

"Forty minutes did you say?"

"Yes."

I pushed Faith's hair up and off her shoulders and behind her head as I leaned down and began laying kisses on her neck, her long delicate throat and onto her bare shoulders. Faith had the most amazing shoulders: broad and strong. Round and firm. She was muscular and fit, accentuated by her tank top. My hands slid down her sides, my thumbs brushing her breasts as they slowly descended the frame of her body. She inhaled sharply.

"Noah . . ."

I loved the way she whispered my name: full of raw desire.

"Faith, why do we fight when this is ever so much better? Promise me, the next time we argue, we will end it like this."

"And in bed?"

"Yes. In bed where nothing else matters but you and me."

"Then, perhaps, we should separate more often."

Still reveling in the afterglow, I had to leave our bed, and drive to the baseball field to pick up our daughter. Janie came bounding toward the car with Darla walking steadily behind her.

" I thought Mom was going to pick me up."

"Yeah, well, she was kind of tired, so I said I would come get you."

"Actually—if it's all right—Darla's going to take me home. We're going to stop at the Dairy Bar for ice cream."

"You'll spoil your appetite."

"Right! I'll be home around five. Is that OK?"

"Back to our house, remember? Mom's already packed your stuff. Everything is in the car."

"Great!"

"So, we'll see you for dinner. We're ordering pizza."

What else would you have after great sex, especially since neither Faith nor I smoke?

"Yep. We'll be there."

So, Darla's coming for dinner, too. Those two are stuck like glue.

When I returned home, Faith was still in bed. She had worn herself out. Sex with Faith was always like a good, well-paced run. Mile after glorious mile filled with sites, sounds, and smells along the way, culminating with a final push: sprinting and heaving to the finish line.

I sat down on the bed next to Faith and rubbed her back, our lovemaking still wafting in the air.

"Faith . . ." I whispered, "Darla is bringing Janie home in time for dinner. You should probably get out of bed now," I chuckled as I shook her a little harder. Faith rose up enough for me to wrap my arms around her naked body. She rested her head on my shoulder.

"Dinner, and then it will be time." she softly whimpered.

"I know . . ."

I can't explain it. When we're with Janie, it's like nothing else exists; yet we both instinctively know that we have to leave with the outgoing tide. We don't question it, even though we have no recollection of where we are headed and what awaits us. I guess it's similar to the way birds know when to begin their migration and are mysteriously guided toward their preordained destinations.

The only way I can begin to make sense of it is to relate it to the way God created everything to have a rhythm. He created the earth and everything on it, and in it, in rhythmic units called yoms, or indeterminate intervals of time. And rhythm sustains life. Human life begins because of the rhythm of a woman's menstrual cycle. The heart beats and blood flows in pulsating rhythms. We breathe air—in and out—in rhythm. The earth circles the sun every three hundred sixty-five and one quarter days. There are two low tides and two high tides every lunar day, which is twenty-four hours and fifty minutes.

Faith and I instinctively knew to return to the boathouse with the outgoing tides, it was natural and the pull was irresistible.

However, once we returned, we remembered everything that had happened, including Janie. We "knew" the past, just as Moses had been given knowledge as he hid in the cleft of the rock and God passed by him.

I am not saying any of this is of God. I am just trying to understand how what I know to be true might reconcile with what was happening to us. Faith had somehow discovered, or had fallen upon, the effects of the tidal rhythms synchronized with the infinite Fibonacci spiral of the sundial, and of course, illuminated and/or culminated through, or by, light.

It was after dark when Faith and I found ourselves seated at the table on the dock.

And as I said, I remembered everything that had happened.

Everything.

Faith had always been passionate, but this new Faith—Janie's mother, the woman I *would have* married—was a tigress. She clearly enjoyed watching me, taunting me, playing me, making me throb and quiver, and spinning me out of control on her terms. I wondered if these were things she had learned from Tyler. But that would have been impossible in the scenario that included Janie. Right? There would have been no Tyler. It would have only been "us."

Don't judge me. Yes, I'm well aware that I should not be dwelling on such things. But, as I keep saying, I am human. I am not perfect, not by a long stretch. Without memory, I'd have no need for a conscience. After all, we know that sex *is* of God. It's what brought us here: rhythmically conjoined bodies.

And let's talk about the gift of sex. It is a blessing, and a curse.

Sex can be beautiful. And intimacy makes two become one.

But sex can also be used for evil. When God handed down his punishment to Eve, he said that men would rule over women. If this was meant as a consequence of Eve's actions, then it could not have meant that man's rule would be in women's best interests. Here, I believe, God introduced sexual injustices to the world. What was meant as beauty became a curse. And, women are abused, beaten, raped, and even die a horrible death because of it.

My eyes met Faith's.

"What are we going to do?" I asked.

"Before I return to Seattle, I am going to leave you the sundial. You will be here and able to drop in on Janie, and then let me know how she's doing."

"You know this is crazy, right? You know we could wake up tomorrow, or the day after you leave, and realize it was all a dream."

"Yes. I know. But I doubt it. This is real, Noah. She's real. The way I love her . . . and loved you . . . is real."

My eyes met hers. I could deny none of it.

"We have to try, for her, for my peace of mind," Faith pleaded.

Faith's eyes turned sad. I struggled not to respond to her or show any emotion. Inside, I was being torn apart. I have a daughter.

A daughter: flesh of my flesh, and bone of my bone.

I absolutely adored Janie, and she thinks I'm the best. (I know that because she told me.) And yes, if I had married Faith, I would have loved her. But honestly, Chrissy and I are soul mates. We are bound together by something that is stronger than children. We share what most people never will in a lifetime. We share the sense of deep loss. A yearning that seeps into every stitch of our fabric. We have learned to survive together, and neither of us would be able to leave the other to go it alone. Chrissy and I sing a song in unison that most people can hear, but certainly cannot understand. That song is the undertone of our life, and we have learned to acknowledge it and arrange our lives around it: Chrissy and I will never have children.

How was I now to continue with this new dimension? This rearrangement? I could never leave Janie. And I could not imagine Faith's sense of loss once she returned to Seattle.

And, one day, soon, Chrissy would have to know. She would have to come with me.

CHAPTER SEVEN

FAITH

The baptism was beautiful. It was surreal standing on the bank of the North East River where I grew up, watching as Noah led Nigel into the lazy current. Waist deep in water, about thirty feet offshore, Noah spoke softly to Nigel. I imagined he was asking Nigel if he was ready, perhaps sharing how proud he was of Nigel's commitment to his "New Life." Then, Noah lifted his voice and made a proclamation on Nigel's behalf.

"The disciple, Peter, said in 1st Peter 3: 'This water symbolizes baptism that now saves you—not the removal of dirt from the body, but the pledge of a clear conscience toward God.' " Noah stopped and looked toward all of us who were witnessing the event and he purposefully and emphatically repeated the last phrase, preaching to "the choir" standing on the riverbank. He repeated, "but the pledge of a clear conscience toward God." Then Noah turned back to Nigel. " 'It saves you by the resurrection of Jesus Christ who has gone into heaven and is at God's right hand—with angels, authorities and power in submission to him.' Nigel, I baptize you in the name of the Father, the Son, and the Holy Spirit."

And with that, Nigel placed a hand over his nose, pinching it closed, and Noah dipped him back and into the water. Raising Nigel back up, the water leapt up around Nigel's body as he thrust his hands high above his head and hollered as one would after scoring the game-winning touchdown.

I am very cynical about religion and all its pomp and circumstance, but even I have to admit that it was a moving experience. Nigel even looked "new."

Nigel stood prouder that afternoon as the food was uncovered and we celebrated down by the river. Nigel's mother made the rounds, hugging and thanking everyone, especially Noah and Chrissy, crowing that they had saved her son. Noah humbly corrected her, stating that Nigel had always been in God's hands. (Noah tossed about a lot of Christian sound bites that day.) She thanked my mother for allowing the baptism to take place in such a lovely setting. Nigel's mother was crying happy tears most of the time. Others might think she was being overdramatic, but I think she was just that happy and relieved, especially to see that many people there in support of her son.

Nigel and his best friend, Emily, eventually sat down on the edge of the dock, each with a plate of food in their lap and their feet in the water. You could tell Emily was a special girl and a good friend to Nigel. I silently pondered the notion that if Janie were here, she and Emily might have been the very best of friends. Janie, too, *is* the type of altruistic girl who stands up and fights for what she believes are indisputable humanitarian causes: things like civil rights, gay rights, the annihilation of child abuse and cruelty to animals. Emily struck me as that kind of person, too.

Noah had Chrissy by his side all afternoon. They politely circulated while everyone was eating and chatting about the beautiful day, God's presence at this occasion, taking prayer requests for family members and friends in need, and listening to people express their fears about what will happen when Carl Harper finds out.

I confess that the more I got to know Chrissy, the more I liked her—and the more I grew jealous of her life. She had Noah, and it was obvious that they were very happy together and made for a good team. She was cheery and optimistic, always looking for the brighter side of every circumstance. She was well-spoken and spoken well of. She could quote the Bible just as readily as Noah. They laughed at the same jokes and innuendos.

Who knew that Christians could have such a witty sense of humor?

They listened intently as others expressed their concerns. She was especially good at consoling those with doubts and worries. And . . . she was beautiful. I'm sure many considered Noah a lucky man and she was his lucky lady. It was easy to see that Chrissy was everything to him.

Biologically, they would never have children, so it seemed they had made God's children their own, and before I came along, that would have been enough for Noah.

As the celebration wound down, a pseudo receiving line formed as attendees exiting the property congratulated Nigel and said their goodbyes to the McKennas and my mother. It then became clear to me that at the end of the day, I had also witnessed the importance, and the value, of "fellowship" among the Christian community.

I also observed that with strong, shared beliefs and convictions came strong opposition. Now that the baptism had been carried out, the concern for Noah among this small group of followers was becoming palpable. I stood by and heard them say things like:

"God bless you and protect you." *(Sound bite!)*

"You did the right thing."

"How do you think the Elders are going to react?"

"I'll pray for you." *(Another sound bite, probably the most overused one that's never carried out.)*

Noah was in trouble. It was just like him to make sacrifices for others. It was just like him to say he wasn't worried.

CHAPTER EIGHT

NOAH

It just so happened that we were in the middle of a teaching series entitled "UnChristian" when everything surrounding Nigel broke loose. The objective of the entire series was to shed light on how the "unchurched" viewed the Christian community. Sunday's message would focus on things like the Church's reputation for being judgmental, hypocritical, and assigning weighted values to sin when the Bible clearly states that all sin is equal. (And, by the way, the Bible also states that the penalty for all sin is the same: Death.) Each message concludes with a reminder of God's infinite grace, which is a gift offered to everyone—no exclusions. Jesus died for *one,* and for *all.*

Some might say that the timing could not have been better. I'm here to tell you that it felt like the timing could not have been worse. The way I lived out what I preached in this series fueled the flames of the Elders, led by Carl Harper. As I delivered the message of God's abundant grace—though somehow the Christian culture had succeeded in placing prerequisites around it—I could see Harper's face growing redder and redder. He was a cannon about ready to fire straight toward the pulpit. At the end of my message, he demonstratively stood and stormed out. I was relieved when he exited the chapel because it was then that I announced that Nigel had been baptized in the river the day before. Some congregants cautiously clapped and timidly cheered, while others remained stone-faced. A very few boldly stood and made a boisterous show of their approval, the same ones who were with us on the riverbank the day before.

After the last hymn, "They Will Know We Are Christians By Our Love," Chrissy, Nigel, and I stood at the back of the church and received the morning's attendees. The brick walls of the small foyer never felt so cold. Some congratulated Nigel and heartily shook his hand. Many more were short with their goodbyes and quickly departed with their spouses and families in tow. Chrissy remained upbeat and animated, blessing everyone, just like any other Sunday. I am sure my sense of failure—failure to break down fortresses and open hearts to God's word—was written all over my face. How do I know this? Because when Faith stepped up with her mother, Faith, of all people, told me to not look so defeated.

Never before had I second-guessed my actions as I did in those two days. Did I fail to reach my congregation by rushing to seize the moment and baptize Nigel? Had I unwittingly fortified their bulwarks of exclusivity by putting them in a position to defend their obstructive convictions? Had I lost the opportunity to guide them through a healthy debate on whether we, the Church, have made it more difficult for someone to be received into our fellowship than welcomed into heaven?"

The baptism split our membership into three distinct groups: those who believe that baptism is for all, those who believe that baptism is reserved only for those who commit to living within a fundamental interpretation of the Bible, and those caught in the middle of the other two fighting factions.

We were now a church in turmoil, and in the end, I was probably going to lose my job.

My parents were spending the weekend on the Nauti-Lass III and had invited Chrissy and me out for the day. This would have been my first opportunity to speak with my mother since learning about Faith's abortion and that my mother had specifically ordered it. However, with Chrissy onboard, there was no chance that I was going to broach the subject.

Faith's father, Mr. Cuthbertson, prior to his death, made me promise never to speak of Faith's pregnancy. It now occurred to me that he must have known what had happened. It was finally dawning on me that everyone was in on it, except me. They thought it was absolutely imperative for me to be kept from the truth. Those closest to me had inadvertently seen to it that I would never become a father and, worse yet, that poor Faith would have to live with the lie and the loss.

Pulling together the pieces and assembling the web of deceitful omission helped me to better understand Faith and why she had refused to see me before I left for Boston University all those years ago. She was trying to protect me from the truth of what had actually taken place.

I had a difficult time being around my parents that day. My gut was twisted into knots and I wanted to pull my mother aside and let her know that what she had done was no longer a secret. I wanted to ask her how she could live with herself knowing that she had robbed me of the one chance I had of becoming a father. That she had denied herself and Dad the gift of a beautiful granddaughter that only Faith could give them. I wanted to tell my mother that I had met Janie and that she was a wonderful young lady, full of spunk and promise, and that she—my mother—had selfishly destroyed the life that was rightfully mine. That she completely disregarded my role as the father. I was a legal adult at the time and had every right to be a part of that decision. The decision should have rested with Faith and me, and no one else. That decision was ours to make, and, in fact, there would have been no decision to be made. My mother had no right to interfere.

My stomach was roiling. I couldn't talk during lunch, served shortly after Chrissy and I had arrived. I buried my thoughts for fear of what might come out of my mouth if I had allowed my anger and regrets to surface.

My mother was all cheery and patronizing, showing off for a new guest onboard. Amelia was Thomas's latest fling. Chrissy kindly played along and pulled out all kinds of information from Amelia. I stewed and wondered what part of Thomas's life Mom had managed to manipulate and permanently alter.

After lunch, everything was stowed away and we headed out for an afternoon cruise. Mom and Dad proudly sat up on the fly bridge while Thomas and Amelia remained on the lower deck with their hips glued together. There wasn't much point in trying to hold a conversation with them over the engine noise, thank goodness.

The North East River was stirred up with all of the boaters heading out for a Sunday afternoon on the water. As we passed the Cuthbertson residence, I was not surprised to see two small figures seated around the table on the dock. I couldn't help but squint and stare. The boathouse behind them looked ominous now, alive with stories to tell.

I couldn't help but wonder what Janie was doing at that moment.

Had we been able to keep her, I wonder what we would have been doing at this particular moment on this particular day?

When we reached our destination, between Bull Mountain and Rocky Point, Dad lowered and set the anchor. When the engines were shut down, Chrissy and I moved to the bow of the boat.

"Everything OK, Noah?" she asked quietly as she slipped an arm under mine and snuggled up against me. "You don't seem yourself today."

"Yeah. I'll be all right."

"Things bothering you about this morning? Carl Harper getting under your skin?"

In my discontent with my mother and my recent wonderings regarding the Cuthbertson boathouse, I had forgotten all about the morning's tension among the congregation.

"Somewhat. He can be a bit of an impulsive hothead, so I worry about Nigel, and I worry about the sentiments of the congregation, and the Board of Elders and how much Harper can influence them."

"Well, you're not supposed to worry about such things. Matthew 6:34. Remember?"

We both recited it in unison, "Do not worry about tomorrow, for tomorrow will worry about itself. Each day has enough trouble of its own."

Chrissy continued, "And you can't add one hour to your life by worrying. Right?"

"Yes, I know. I know," I said, doubly acknowledging her second reference to the book of Matthew. "In fact, worrying just seems to make my day grow longer."

In a rare public display of affection, I reached over and grabbed Chrissy around the waist and held her close to me, kissing her with full of adoration, cloaking my guilt and unspoken apology. Yes, I was beginning to keep secrets from Chrissy and I hated myself for it.

I was upset with Faith for recently putting me in this position, yet glad that she had shared Janie with me.

I resented my mother for what she had done.

But above all, I was so grateful that Chrissy was in my life, something that may not have happened had my mother not convinced Faith to go to New York. What a contradiction of terms. What a mess.

Life is so messy.

Would it have happened anyway . . . just not this way?

Pastors don't have all the answers, and they certainly get tied in knots just like everyone else, maybe more. There is such pressure on pastors to have all the answers. There is even more pressure exerted on them and their families to live perfect, sinless lives. To practice what we preach without exception, with a grateful, saintly smile on our faces, to be perfect role models, everywhere, all the time.

Chrissy laid her head on my shoulder and sighed, "I love you, Noah McKenna. You're a good man with a good heart. And when things get tough, and you fight back with truth, whether it's the easy way out, or not, I find it sexy as hell."

"Sexy as hell, huh?" I repeated, somewhat wearily.

The "hell" of it was that I was now withholding deep truths from the most important person in my life, and it was making me miserable.

I looked around the yacht. Everyone seemed pre-occupied.

Maybe now is the time to tell Chrissy?
No, not here. She has the right to hear it in private, not in front of my family where there is no escape.

Unknowingly, my shoulders slumped in resignation and I was looking down rather than out across the water as I should have been.

Chrissy is quick to notice such things.

"Noah, whatever it is, you've got to let it go."

FAITH

Monday morning and time was running out. Soon, I would be flying back to Seattle, leaving Noah to keep up the visits with Janie on his own. I believed he was my only hope.

Late Sunday afternoon, I got it into my head to see if I could make the journey back to Janie from a location other than the boathouse. Perhaps there was a way to visit her from Seattle? I took the sundial up to the Turkey Point Lighthouse. From atop the one hundred foot bluff, I knew I could capture the late afternoon sun reflecting off the water. I was hoping that I could recreate the same conditions that had transported me when I was in the boathouse: low tide, strong light, and the sundial in my hand.

Standing in several different sites on the Point, including the gallery of the lighthouse, my attempts to join Janie repeatedly failed. Sadly, I was ultimately convinced that all conditions, including the boathouse, had to be met without exception. It was only from that one spot, where Noah and I had made love, and Janie was conceived, that I could be transported to her. Therefore, there would be no means of travel once I returned to Seattle.

After my failed attempts, of which there were many, I quickly retreated back down the dirt trail to my car. I sped back to my mother's home and ran down to the dock. There was still enough time remaining in the outgoing tide to visit Janie, if only for a little while.

She was such a joy to be near. A smile spread across my face just thinking about her. I knew that the mere sight of her had the power to extinguish all my cares. When I was with her, my firstborn, she was also my direct link to what life would have been with Noah. In that life, he would have been mine.

Consequently, because I had "found" her, I would now miss her and everything about her when I landed in Seattle at the end of the week. The sound of her voice, her laugh, her smile and wit, the way she would run her fingers through her hair to give it lift, her wide and telling eyes, the scent of her that lingered in her bedroom. Janie was becoming a beautiful, young adult. She was in the prime of her life and I adored watching her maneuver through the landmines of her youth. And when one detonated under her feet, I was always so proud of the way she would pick herself up and carry on. Janie struggled like any other teenager, but she would always find a silver lining in whatever ordeal she was facing. And even though I hadn't been with her every day, I knew these things about her. For when I *was* with her, I had been with her all along. Also, when I *was* with Janie, I had been with Noah. It was an indescribable sensation to live the life that could have been mine.

You would think, then, that when I did have the opportunity to visit with her, when all conditions were met, that I would run to her and smother her with hugs and kisses. That I would be like a mother when she captures the first glimpse of her child-soldier returning home after a long tour of duty overseas. However, my visits were nothing like that. Yes, I would stand back and marvel at her like any other parent would, filled with moments of wonder. Yet when I returned to her, it was as if a day had never been lost. Sadly, though, when I was *there*, I had no recollections of my life in Seattle. No knowledge of Tyler, Charlie, or Maddie. They were non-existent when I was with Janie.

That was the scary part.

What if the time comes when I can't return "home" after one of my visits? Will I lose Charlie and Maddie?
What if the shell breaks or I somehow lose it?
What if I have an accident and can't return to the boathouse in time to get back?

What if something happens to Charlie or Maddie while I'm "away?"

So many *"what ifs"* in my life . . .

Ironically, I had been given the opportunity to see my greatest *"what if,"* and you would think that that would have put an end to it. But no, it served to plague me with new, and more numerous, hypothetical questions.

It never seemed to end. The answers only created more questions.

Is there no such thing as a life without the affliction of "what ifs?"

I had been granted the ability to experience the road not taken. I was able to see what would have been had I done nothing and plowed ahead with what I thought was my doom. What had haunted me for sixteen years was now visible and viable. It was a gift, and a curse. It brought me great joy to see her, and soon it would produce enormous amounts of pain when I returned to Seattle, more so than ever before.

I had seen the life that Noah had wanted, and at this late juncture, as it were, I would stand at a crossroad that would forever pull me apart. Whatever relief I had found in my discovery had only succeeded to grieve me more knowing that if I *had* followed Noah's plan, I would not have Charlie and Maddie . . . and Tyler.

Isn't that the way of life's extremes, where one end meets the other? Have you ever cried tears of joy? Have you ever been in so much pain that you eventually go so numb that you feel nothing at all? Have you ever loved so much that you loathe what it's done to you? Have you ever felt like you can't live with someone; yet you can't live without them? How about the more you know, the less you understand? Or, one needs light to see; yet too much light is blinding.

Yes, I had been granted full knowledge with the ability to live within it. Yet, soon it would break my heart.

This truth was not going to set me free. Oh, I would be free of my hypothetical wonderings of *"what if"* I had made a different choice sixteen years ago. But now I would have to live with the absolute awareness of something I had given up. Perhaps, I would have been better off not knowing.

Maybe this was all for Noah?

No. That's a load of crap, too. A feeble rationalization to ease my guilt. I am not sure of my reasons for sharing this experience with Noah. I fear that if I could be perfectly honest with myself, part of me did it to offer Noah something that Chrissy could not. Was it a callous attempt to upend Noah's relationship with Chrissy? He has a child—a daughter. He must now choose to keep it a secret, or share it with Chrissy. At this point, it would be easier for Noah to believe there is no God than to deny Janie. He has seen Janie, touched her, shared conversations with her. Either way, he, too, gains and loses from this new revelation.

I should probably return to Seattle and then smash the shell to pieces so everything goes back to the way it was. But there is no return. There is no undoing of knowledge gained, or truth made known. Noah would never deny God, and he certainly can't deny Janie.

I had to find Noah and give him the shell. He would have to make the journey on his own and assure me that he could, and would, visit with Janie as often as possible. I even wanted him to send me pictures, if he could find a way to return with them. I questioned whether or not I could, or should, send Janie notes or letters?

When Noah did make future trips to visit Janie, would I even be *"there"*? And how would that be possible? It dawned on me that I had never seen Noah *"there"* unless he had traveled with me from the boathouse.

My head was swimming with questions and my heart was drowning. And through it all, I missed Charlie and Maddie more than ever. I hated to leave North East, but

I couldn't wait to get back to Seattle to see my babies, to be with Tyler.

Life was never going to be the same for me because from that point on I could never "unsee" or "unknow" what I had given up.

I finally reached Noah around noon. Chrissy had answered the phone on the first two calls, so I hung up. The third time was the charm.

"Who is this?" Noah demanded, highly annoyed.

"Noah, it's me. Faith. Come to the house when you can. I want you to take the sundial. I need to know that you can make the journey on your own before I leave for Seattle."

And then I hung up. If he chose to, Noah could tell Chrissy it was a prank call.

More importantly, I hoped that he would follow through with my request.

NOAH

As soon as Faith's call disconnected, I shouted into the silenced receiver, "Stop calling here!" And then I hung up, slamming the receiver into its cradle.

"Hopefully, we won't be bothered by them again," I playacted for Chrissy's benefit.

And that's how my omissions and lies were solidified. I was already down the slippery slope and had taken the plunge. I had no idea how long I could get away with it before I was eventually found out. That was the scariest part of all. Chrissy was very perceptive. She could read people as if they were open books in large print. I was putting our marriage on the line for something Faith had convinced me was real and mine. I had started down the path of escalating untruths for the sake of a former lover and a daughter who could have been pure fantasy. I had no idea what I was doing. But what was done was done and could not be reversed. I had stepped over the line and the potential fallout was now hanging over my head like a guillotine. Worst of all, the longer it went on, I knew the build up of falsifications would eventually snowball. When Chrissy found out—and she would—she would be crushed, demolished that I had been hiding something that had so much sway over me. There, in my own home with my beloved wife sitting before me at the lunch table, my snap decision would break her. The burden I had latched onto was causing my spine to collapse beneath the weight of the inevitable. I had lied in order to obtain something Chrissy could never give me: a child. Chrissy would be devastated to think that I had rushed into some concocted arrangement with a former lover, leaving her behind and out of something that meant so much to me. She would think that all of my past reassurances regarding the impossibility of our becoming parents had been iced-over, shallow pretenses.

I would probably lose her. Even if she considered staying in the marriage, it would alter our relationship forever.

Needless to say, I didn't go to the Cuthbertson's as Faith had demanded.

Mondays and Tuesdays were my typical days off. In the last two years, Chrissy had managed to have her classes structured around my schedule and we now had two consecutive days a week to ourselves. Barring any emergencies within our church and community, I was going to spend them with Chrissy.

Fortunately, Faith was due to depart for Seattle in several days and my life would hopefully return to some semblance of normalcy once she boarded her flight. I would ask God to forgive me for never sharing with Chrissy what had happened in the past week. I would shoulder the damage and never allow it to come near her. I would do my best to insure that Chrissy would never perceive a change in me, or that Janie even exists. I might even cease the visits to Janie and suffer the heartache to spare my wife the agony.

"Chrissy, let's get away. Let's take the next two days and go on a little mini vacation."

"Who was on the phone?"

Chrissy studied my agitation.

"Did that call have something to do with Nigel? Do you really think it is wise for us to leave the area right now?"

"Yes, especially now. I'll leave a forwarding number on the church answering machine. We won't go far. Just far enough. How about the Robert Morris Inn, in Oxford? No phone, no TV, just you and me."

"You just said you were going to leave a forwarding number on the answering machine at church?"

"I'll have all messages taken at the front desk at the inn. I'll return the calls when it's convenient for both of us. How's that?"

I really needed to get away and take Chrissy with me. I needed to be in a place where I could redirect my attention and concentrate on my vows and promises to Chrissy, and to my God.

All during college and after receiving my divinity degree, I thought the North East River was where I wanted to spend the rest of my life. At the time, all I wanted was to reconnect with Faith. I had prayed for that day for years. I had prayed that we would find a way to reunite and take up the journey that I had felt certain was meant for us. That was before I had met Chrissy. And now, my former and long abandoned prayer had been answered in ways I had never imagined and the answer was becoming my biggest nightmare. Faith, though well meaning, was now the cause of my underlying misery. And to my great despair, I realized that in His wisdom, God had also answered a second prayer, just not the way I had wanted it:

I was a father.

Or, Faith and I are insane.

CHRISSY

Looking back on it now, I realize that I should have trusted my gut instinct. Faith's return to North East was indeed going to impact our lives.

My friends, the ones who are natives to the area, were right to point her out in church, suggesting that she and Noah had "history." I remember how the back of my neck prickled as I glanced up at Noah, still standing in the pulpit. I watched as he searched for her among the congregants that Sunday. I remember, now, being less than happy when I learned that he had given Faith a ride to Turkey Point on his way to rescue Nigel. I remembered how Faith was lost in thought during lunch in her mother's home, and how Faith had followed Noah down the hall where a whispered conversation between the two of them took place.

Then, there was this sudden need to take a mini vacation in the midst of trouble within the church. This one action was so far out of Noah's realm of characteristic behaviors that it stuck out as the most peculiar. Normally, he would have been buried in prayer, solemn prayer times that would have included me. Conversely, when we did pray together, his prayers had become scattered, interrupted by distractions that were swirling around in his head, and in his heart. Somehow, it all seemed to center around Faith's return to the area. It was becoming more obvious that his troubles within the church were being eclipsed by another, bigger distraction named Faith Cuthbertson Livingston.

Noah made the call, and the Robert Morris Inn had a room available for us. After hanging up the phone, he exhaled the breath he had been holding.

"C'mon, Baby, we're outta here!"

It didn't even sound like him. He was giddy with relief, filled with renewed energy. His determination grew resolute and he became the commander before his army. And I, his one loyal trouper, could now clearly see the enemy. I was the lowest rank on the field, subservient to things that to-date were out of my control. Noah was running from *her*. We were not going into battle. We were retreating from it. And, his surrender would be imminent when we returned to fight another day. I could lose him forever.

Noah began packing in a hurry, claiming he wanted to make the most of our time away.

All of my red flags were raised to full staff. Warning bells were sounding in my head. This sudden getaway was not about us. It had nothing to do with Nigel or Carl Harper. It was about his feelings for Faith. Something had happened, or was about to happen. I stood frozen in the kitchen, mentally searching for every explanation that could possibly disprove my theory. Dejectedly, the more I reviewed the events of the past week, the more evidence I accrued, exposing the truth: Noah was beholden to Faith. They were colluding in some sort of arrangement and were keeping secrets from me. My mind was racing frantically through a maze of thoughts that could only end in disaster.

Packed and ready to go, Noah returned to the kitchen to find me leaning over the counter with my head planted in my hands.

"Chrissy, c'mon. Time's a-wastin'. You need to get packed."

I didn't move. Not even a shift in stance.

"Chrissy? Are you OK?"

"Sure . . . sure. I think we should go."

"Well, then, let's get you packed and we'll get on the road."

I straightened up and turned to look at the man I had married. The one whose promises I trusted to the ends of the earth. The one into whose hands I had placed my life. Looking through the lens of my latest revelation, I could see the worry in his eyes and feel the panic in his restlessness. It confirmed my worst imaginings.

NOAH

The farther away North East appeared in my rearview mirror, the better I felt. Chrissy and I would get to spend a couple of days together in Oxford, away from the pressures that were mounting back home. It was the right thing to do. I needed to stay away from Faith. *We* needed to stay away from Faith. At this point in our lives, Faith could only bring us trouble.

Janie . . .

I shook my head as if trying to dislodge the thought. The dream. None of it was true. Either it couldn't be, or I wouldn't let it be. Because if it *were* true, then I have a daughter. If I have a daughter, then I had some other life that didn't include Chrissy. The implications seemed enormous. Pure insanity.

It can't be true.

As we traveled in silence, I mentally searched the Bible for evidence of such miraculous dreams and journeys. Example after example filled my recollections from the Old and New Testaments. One of God's main means of communication was through dreams and angels. And, God is, after all, in the business of miracles. Recorded events in the Bible, many more on the battlefields in history books, proclaimed in sports arenas every day, in hospitals around the world, and visible to us in our everyday lives, we are witnesses to God's handiwork.

But this?

Perhaps it was a dream rather than some performed miracle with no logical, scientific evidence or explanation.

But it seemed *so* real.

A miracle? A first of its kind?

I looked over at Chrissy. She, too, was lost in thought. I reached across and placed my hand on her knee, convinced that lately I had not been affectionate enough toward her.

"What are you thinking about?"

"You."

"Me?"

"Yes. You and me."

I waited for her to elaborate. But she didn't. She just turned her head away, staring hard out the passenger window as if mesmerized by the scenery passing by.

I took her hand from her lap.

"Chrissy, I know the past several days have been tough. That's why I thought we should get away. I miss you."

"You miss me? I've been right here. Where have you been, Noah? You're the one who's been absent."

"I've been right here."

"No. You haven't." Chrissy proceeded to cut right to the chase, an unfamiliar move that knocked me off balance. "Ever since we had lunch at the Cuthbertson's, you've been distant. Preoccupied. And it has nothing to do with Nigel or Carl Harper. You've shared everything with me regarding that whole situation, including taking Faith along with you to the lighthouse."

"Then what is it? What's bothering you?" I asked, stepping right into the hornet's nest.

"It's Faith. Ever since she cornered you back in their hallway while her mother and I waited by the door, things have changed. You've changed. And now, this. You're running. You're running away from her. What happened, Noah? Tell me, please. What has happened between the two of you? Your silence and secrets are killing me."

Admittedly, in the last week, I had given a lot of thought as to what I would do when this particular moment had arrived. I knew that ultimately the truth would start to unravel or would wear me down. I also knew that Chrissy would probably figure it out long before I was ready to talk about it, which would have been never. Thinking I could isolate Chrissy from the craziness surrounding Faith was pure folly. And now the tears were forming in Chrissy's eyes, all due to my reckless behavior. Chrissy had put on a strong front, but now, in the car, with her question floating between us, she could no longer contain her suspicions and they were about to overwhelm us. She had been holding back a tidal wave of emotions.

We probably drove another half-mile in silence while I searched for an explanation that wouldn't sound absurd or hurt her any further.

And then I recalled making love to Faith.

OK. Let me stop right here and confess that if I were to say that this was one of the rare times I had recalled making love to Faith, I'd be lying. Of course, I had thought of it ... OK, replayed it ... many times over. Over and over. It was, sadly, something I obviously treasured. After all, Faith was the reason I had moved to North East. Yet, it was making me sick as well. Of all the secrets I was keeping from Chrissy, this was by far the worst.

But what if it *was* all some sort of dream? That I had only imagined it?

See? That's the problem. If it's only a dream, why should I speak of it and open Pandora's box? Why make something of nothing? Are we meant to share every dream with our spouses? Is it considered concealment or lying if we don't disclose such delusions or fantasies?

But, to be honest, I am fairly certain that it wasn't a dream. If it was just a dream, why would I be spending so much time worrying about it and trying to convince myself otherwise? If I could positively deny that one act—the lovemaking—then I could probably live with everything else ... and so could Chrissy. But, I knew it was real. A sober man cannot deny his actions. I remembered everything. Every detail. It haunts me like any ruinous act that brings one down with the fulfillment of thirsty pleasure. I knew without a doubt that I had made love to Faith. That I had been in another bed. I could feel the lingering effects of exertion. I could taste her sweet juices on my lips. . . smell her arousal . . . and it was not Chrissy.

My head spun at the memory of the hours spent making love so new, yet so familiar.

And then there's Janie, the innocent one. Sixteen and alive, and beautiful. She called me "Daddy." She hugged me and brought to me a dimension of love and exhilaration I had never known before. And the truth was, even if I could let go of Faith, I could never let go of Janie.

"Turn the car around!"

Chrissy's sharp words stung and snatched me from my muted musings.

"Chrissy?"

"You heard me. Turn the car around, Noah. I mean it. We're going home."

"Look, I know you're upset. Let's get to . . ."

"No. We're going back to North East, and you're going to deal with whatever it is that you're running from. Clearly you can't tell me what it is, so you're going to face it. Alone."

Alone? I don't like the sound of that.

"Chrissy, I really think that . . ."

"No. We're going back."

FAITH

Recognizing the sound of his footsteps coming down the dock, I turned to gaze upon his tall slender physique and his wind-blown hair. In his element, the outdoors, Noah always looked like a Greek god. I wondered if Chrissy knew just how lucky she was. A pair of Aviators cloaked his piercing blue eyes, making it impossible to read the mood he was in, or the reason for his visit. I could only assume it was due to the numerous messages I had left.

I stood as he approached. My acknowledgement of his presence immediately stopped him in his tracks. He removed his shades. Defeat. It was written all over his face.

"Faith, I can't do this anymore. I can't see you . . . or Janie . . . ever again."

I remained silent. A wrecking ball broke loose from its chain and fell to the pit of my stomach, almost knocking me to my knees. I braced myself for further explanation.

Noah rubbed his forehead and exhaled heavily, readying himself for the question I already knew was coming.

"Faith, did we really make love?"

"Yes. We did. As husband and wife."

Noah turned his back to me. He couldn't look at me. His spine and shoulder muscles working hard to keep his stature erect.

I took a step toward him.

"Noah, what happened between us is something I will cherish forever. I needed to know that you would have never given up on me. That you would have been willing to face life's ups and downs with me and still continue to love me."

"NO! STOP IT! JUST STOP IT! THAT'S JUST CRUEL AND UNFAIR!" Noah turned back toward me and let loose with torrents of anger. "You left me. You took Janie from me. You cut her right out of my life. I suffered for years thinking I had caused you enormous amounts of pain. I carried that guilt. But, I also carried hope, the hope that there was enough love remaining to one day repair the damage I had done. That's why I came back here, to North East. I came for you, Faith. But, I was too late. It was your father who told me. He was a very kind and forgiving man, your dad.

"Then, thank God, I met Chrissy. She is everything to me, Faith. EVERYTHING. And now you show up and introduce me to a daughter I never knew I had. One that I now know everything about, filling me with memories and feelings I can't erase, yet I can't hold on to or share with the most important person in my life."

"You can share them with me . . ." As soon as the words left my mouth, I knew that what I had implied was wrong, terribly wrong, especially when seen through Noah's eyes. It was a moment when my words traveled faster than my brain could process. It was far too easy a thing for me to say.

"I have to let her go, Faith, because of all the people involved here. It's not right. I have to let it go."

"I'm sorry, Noah. I thought . . ."

"No, you didn't think. You didn't think this through."

"I DID! I THOUGHT OF YOU! I thought you'd want to know. I thought you would be ecstatic to know Janie. To know you have a daughter."

"Then where is she, Faith? Is she here? If I have a daughter, then why do I have to go through some crazy gyrations to see her? How do I even know she's mine?"

I should have been insulted and angry by his assault of my character, but I wasn't. I felt as though I deserved some sort of harsh rebuke, as though I had had it coming to me.

"Because you know," I replied softly.

Noah didn't respond.

"Are you really going to give her up?" I asked.

Noah didn't answer.

"OK, Noah. Whatever you decide, I'll understand. God knows I've done enough damage for one lifetime."

Noah looked at me.

"It wasn't your fault, Faith." His eyes contained the very same sadness I walked away from sixteen years ago in the diner parking lot.

"I'm sorry, Noah. I'm sorry it didn't work out for us—the three of us. I'm so very sorry."

Noah didn't reciprocate with any sentiments. Not a word.

"I leave for Seattle Friday evening. You know where to find me if you change your mind."

NOAH

Faith brushed right past me, leaving me to stand on the dock, alone, abandoning me once again as she had done all those years ago. And the reality of giving up Janie sank deep. I would not be able to visit her again without Faith willing it, for Faith still retained possession of the sundial and unless I did something, it was returning to Seattle with her.

Maybe it's for the best.

I remained on the dock for almost another thirty minutes, evaluating all the possible options, including coming clean with Chrissy. If I could make Chrissy understand, perhaps she would take the journey with me. Surely Faith would allow that, considering that it would be a better solution than never seeing or hearing about Janie again, or at least not until her next return to North East.

However, if I did take Chrissy *"there,"* then what relation would she have with Janie? With me? In Janie's world, I was married to Faith. Then, to make matters worse, upon our return, Chrissy would remember all that she had seen and had learned. We would not be able to undo what had been done. We would carry it with us for all our remaining days. I could not in all good conscience fill Chrissy's head with all of those feelings and memories, the ones that I now carry. I could not expose Chrissy to a place where she was anything less than the most important person in my life.

I walked to the end of the dock, past the weathered boathouse, and sat down on the very edge of the splintered wood overlooking the lazy expanse of calm water that was licking the pilings below me. Gulls circled above and cawed over the hum of a fishing boat heading up river. I began to pray in silence.

"Dear Father in Heaven, Creator of all things, the Author and Guardian of my life, the One who knows me

better than I know myself. Please, hear me in my time of need . . . my dire need. I need You now more than ever before, for Your thoughts are greater than my thoughts, and neither are Your ways my ways.

I must make a heavy decision within days. This is nothing like anything I have ever faced before.

Father, I don't even know if this is real. Is this real? Is this a miracle at Your hands? How can I know? Have I searched Your word adequately? For I have found no answers. I have begged You every day and night for Your guidance and You have not answered me. Please, please . . . I need to know what to do.

"If any of this is true, then I have sinned in the most egregious of ways. I have betrayed my wife. I've committed adultery.

At that moment, visions of Faith wrapped around me overwhelmed my concentration. I recalled the way her body absorbed mine and two became one. I could hear her heady moans and soft coos as I brought her to a slow grinding climax.

"What have I done? You alone have the power to take this from me."

I now knew the guilt of an adulterer. I also knew their affliction, their desire to return to the very thing that was going to send them to ruin and destroy the lives of the very people who mattered most to them. My body curled as every muscle constricted with the pain of such poisonous thoughts and memories.

"How am I to love my daughter—if I have a daughter? Do I truly have a daughter?

"How do I restore the sanctity of my marriage? How do I return to the place where none of this has happened? Please, I beg you, please protect Chrissy from this. She's done nothing to deserve any of this. And, she so desperately wanted children . . ."

And then, as if struck by lightning, I knew that I indeed *had* a daughter. Whether Faith had kept the baby, or had aborted it, I had a daughter, and sooner or later, here, or on the other side of heaven, I would have met her.

"Why? Why do this while my feet are still planted on this earth? And why is Chrissy the one to pay the price and face the consequences? I would have kept Janie . . . I would have cherished every moment with her. You know that. You know how heartbroken I was when I thought Faith had lost the baby. You know I would have stayed with her. You know I would have given the world for Janie . . . had I been given the chance."

But, now, I did know Janie.
Was I being given a second chance?

"For Your ways are not my ways . . . Your thoughts are greater than my thoughts . . ."

And I knew I had to see her. I had to see Janie again, if only to find the answers, or say my goodbyes, for now.

The tide suddenly turned and began running out swift and strong. The sky became unsettled, dark with dense clouds moving toward me from the west. Above them thunderheads were roiling as they approached the Eastern Shore. I turned around to face the Cuthbertson house, to reconsider one more visit with Faith's help. That's when I saw the soft glow coming from the old boathouse. And as the sky's dark ceiling dropped over my head, the light intensified inside the decrepit shed. And yes, in my gut, I was terrified.

"Noah! You should probably think about coming into the house!" Faith shouted from her stance at the top of the slope. She was pointing toward the west. "There's a storm coming."

I looked again at the boathouse. The light was continuing to intensify. The wind picked up and skated across the surface of the river creating a fine silver chop that would eventually stir the depths.

"No! Grab the sundial. We have to go," I yelled back in reply. "Now! It's time to go!"

FAITH

Noah, with a forcefulness that I recognized from years long gone, demanded that we go. He was thoroughly committed. Though my concern for the escalating storm was reaching a high, I ran back into the house, the screen door slamming behind me. Sprinting into my room, I grabbed the sundial from my nightstand.

The sudden drop in atmospheric pressure made it known that this storm was going to be a doozy. We would have to move fast.

While I was in the house, Noah made his way to the top of the incline in case he would have to hustle me along. As soon as I flew back out through the screen door, causing it to slam behind me again, we heard the first low rumble of thunder.

"C'mon, we've got to move fast," Noah coaxed as he took my hand and together we ran down the embankment toward the dock.

The wind velocity had increased to the point where it was even more difficult to pull open the boathouse door, scraping and twisting along the dock boards as it went. As soon as the opening was wide enough for us to slip through, we forced our way in.

"Noah, you're sure about this?" I asked as I turned toward him, the storm pushing its way toward us.

His eyes were wild. His jaw was set in the way I had only seen when he was intent on restraining his passion.

I took the shell and held it up so we could see into its intricate spiral. As air began leaving our lungs, there was a loud explosion. In the din of my spinning surroundings I heard Noah shout:

"Faith, wait!"

The dock shook and another bomb went off, somewhere very nearby.

"Faith! Stop!"

I felt Noah's hand leave mine and he was gone.

CHAPTER NINE

FAITH

When I arrived, I was lying on the floor. My throat was on fire. I was choking on hot acidic particles that were filling the vacuum created by the severe spin of travel. Dizzy and suffocating on the dirty air, I crawled along the floor of the boathouse in the hope of finding oxygen and perhaps a line of sight below the smoke and ash. Thunder roared across the water culminating with a whip-snapping crack. My ears rang and my eyes, already stinging from the irritated atmosphere, snapped shut with fear.

Rain suddenly began pouring down in buckets, knocking the smoke to the ground. The torrents of water were heavy and perceptibly impenetrable, substantially blocking my vision. However, it was only momentary. As it began to subside, I could hear the sirens in the distance. I crawled out of the boathouse and turned the corner. A scene opened up before me, as if a curtain had been drawn back on a stage just beyond my front row seat. My mother's house was fully engulfed in flames.

The fire engines began arriving, winding down the swells of their alarms as they made their approach. The rising steam and falling rain now flashed with reflections of bright pulsating reds, whites, and blues. Janie came running through the scrim of smoke and steam.

"Mom! Mom! Are you all right?" Janie screamed as she ran down the dock toward me. "Did you get hit?"

"Hit?" I asked, somewhat dazed.

"Were you hit? Are you OK?"

"Huh?"

"By lightning. Were you hit?"

"No . . . What about you? Are you OK, Janie?"

"Yes. I'm fine. Everyone is fine."

"Where's your father? Your grandmother?"

"They're OK. Dad carried Grandmom out of the house. She's going to be fine."

"Jesus! What happened?" I asked, as Janie helped me to my feet.

"The house was struck by lightning. When we got here, Dad ran in and carried Grandmom out. She apparently fell or tripped on something when she tried to get out by herself. We've been looking for you."

"I'm fine," I reaffirmed as I stood up with Janie's help and gathered her into my arms, wrapping a hand around the back of her head and pulling her to my shoulder. Tears began streaming from my eyes as I realized that we had had a close brush with death.

"It's OK, Mom. We're going to be OK," my beautiful daughter reassured me.

I held my dear sweet teenage girl in my arms, cradling her as if she were a baby.

"C'mon, Mom, let's go find Dad and Grandmom. They'll be relieved to see you." Janie suggested as she wiggled free from my grip.

Noah immediately intercepted us as we staggered off the dock,.

"Faith! Oh, dear God, thank you."

Noah clasped my body into his and held me tighter than he had in years.

"Jesus, I thought I'd lost you. I searched everywhere around the house. Your mother couldn't remember where you were or when she'd last seen you," he sputtered, coughing between his words.

Noah held me, silently, longingly, placing a lingered kiss on the top of my head, his grimy, smoky face buried in my hair. Resting in the strength of his chest, I felt at peace. A tranquil sensation flowed over me from my head to my toes. We had survived, and Noah was here with us.

"Faith," Noah whispered, "we should get back to your mom. She's worried sick about you."

Making our way up the incline, we were directed around the fire equipment and toward the front of the house where we found my mother. Someone had graciously provided her with a lawn chair to sit on and an umbrella to cover her head. For someone who had just seen her house blown apart, she looked relatively calm in the midst of her charred and ash-soaked surroundings.

We stood and watched as water from the fire trucks, and a steady rain from the sky, continued to douse the house that was once a home. The receding sounds of thunder had moved past us and were echoing back from the east. The loud persistent idling of truck engines and generators hummed in the background, occasionally interrupted by the vociferous commands and radio communications of the first responders. Spotlights from the engines illuminated the damage—the near total destruction.

My dad had been notified. He immediately closed the store and was on his way.

Noah and I invited my parents to come stay with us, but they elected to accept the invitation of a church friend. Noah, Janie, and I returned to our cozy home and stayed up well into the night. Powered by adrenaline, we collaborated our stories. As far as we could piece together, my mother was inside, in the kitchen, when the lightning bolt struck the house. Noah and Janie were returning from Janie's dentist appointment when Noah's pager went off. He then, knowingly, sped to the address. When the lightning had struck, I was down on the dock, watching the storm come across the river, as I had always loved to do.

"I can't imagine what it was like for your mom to be in that house when that bolt of lightning struck. It was so loud, I nearly drove off the road and we were at least five miles away. It's a wonder she's alive," Noah speculated.

"Mom, I would have jumped off the dock if I were you!" Janie laughed. "Do you remember any of it?"

"No, not really. I remember being frightened by something. But I also remember feeling elated. It's hard to describe what that amount of energy in the atmosphere feels like. And, I do remember the hairs on my arms standing up just before the strike. Next thing I knew, I was flat out on the floor and everything tingled. My entire body was energized. I just can't explain it."

"Well, thank God everyone is OK. It's a miracle no one was hurt," Noah reaffirmed.

We all settled into bed well after midnight. Noah spooned up against my back, his body wrapped around mine. It felt so good to have all of us under the same roof, safe and sound.

Sleep never eluded Noah. His warm body married into mine as his soft breath kissed the back of my head assuring me of his presence. I, on the other hand, lay wide-awake. Something wasn't right. Something had been left undone. In a flash, my eyes flew open. I realized my mistake. In all the confusion and rush to rejoin my mom, I had failed to collect the sundial. At some point, it must have slipped from my hands. I had to retrieve it before someone else found it.

I shifted slightly so I could reach my arm across the bed to read the alarm clock. It was enough to stir Noah who responded by rolling over onto his other side. It was three in the morning. I had to get to the sundial before someone else discovered it. I prayed it had not fallen into the water.

Driving your car in your pajamas is such a rush. It's like doing something naughty or insane, something your parents would disapprove of. It makes one feel young again, like a kid when you could run around the yard half naked on a summer's day, the cool air kissing your butt, and no one cared.

I pulled into the darkened driveway. Nothing looked the same. Even the tires of my car sounded different as they slowly rolled across the wet gritty residue left behind. There were no lights and the moon was casting unfamiliar shadows created by the burnt out shell of what remained on the property. The fire police had taped off the area, so I had to park farther up the hill.

Upon shutting off the ignition, I could hear night creatures and the faint sound of water moving across the pilings on the river. Without the standing walls of the house as an obstruction, everything sounded louder, closer. Lights across the river that were only visible from the dock were now exposed from the top of the drive. When opening my car door, I was slapped with the unpleasant acrid smell of drenched ash and burnt wood. The ground was still wet, covered with hidden puddles formed by the deep chaotic tire ruts that had been carved into the muddy sand by the fire trucks and heavy emergency equipment. I couldn't even tell you how many fire companies had been called out.

No doubt about it, finding my way down to the dock and the boathouse was going to be an adventure. I left my car's headlights on which only helped for half the distance because of the slope. By the time I made it down to the dock, the headlights were shining way above my head. But I thought it would be enough to guide me and keep me from falling off the dock and into the water.

It was excitingly eerie being there alone and in my PJs at three in the morning without another soul around. A very light breeze was coming off the water, which offered a respite from the sooty air. The water quietly kissed the pilings beneath my feet, a song of ages past. I recalled the night Noah and I went skinny dipping right off that very dock. Too embarrassed to strip down above the surface of the water, we had removed our underwear once our bodies were submerged below the surface.

I was tempted. After all, I was only wearing a nightshirt and a robe. But, commonsense prevailed. One should never swim alone. Plus, it would seem offensive to find pleasure at the site of such devastation. Besides, I had to find the sundial and get back home before Noah woke up.

It didn't take long to locate the shell. It was waiting for me on the floor of the boathouse, just beyond the opening of the door. When I picked it up, the tide shifted and the light was blinding. It was time to leave and return to the life I had chosen sixteen years before.

CHAPTER TEN

FAITH

I remember everything, as if I had never left.

The blast had blown apart two-thirds of the house. Pieces of shingles, siding, and debris had been flung across the sloping yard like confetti.

Everything was dark. There were no lights to guide me.

I recalled Noah letting go of my hand and rushing back up the hill, calling out to my mother.

Neither had emerged from the house.

No . . . NO . . .

"NOAH! NOAH!" I screamed. "MOM!"

I started running. My legs were wobbly with fear. NOAH! MOM! Where are you?"

No response returned from either one.

As I got closer to the house, the evidence indicating the ferocity of the blast was overwhelming. Nothing was left of the kitchen. Half of the family room was gone. Most of the roof had been blown off and what was left was in flames and being rained upon. I collapsed in horror and began crawling toward the rubble when I found one of my mother's favorite slippers, her foot still in it.

I remember all of it.

I have no idea how long I was out. When I came to, I was being loaded into an ambulance. Two paramedics were asking me my name and where I lived. Men in helmets and rescue gear were rushing past us.

"Faith Livingston. I live here. No . . .I mean Seattle. I live in Seattle, but I'm visiting my mother. She . . . lives . . . My mother. Where's my mother? Did you find Noah? Pastor Noah McKenna?

No one answered my questions.

Tyler, with Charlie and Maddie in tow, caught the first flight out of Seattle to Philadelphia and then rented a car to travel the final leg to North East. My sister, Hope, and her husband, Drew, who were still out of the country on business, had been located in London and would soon be on the first flight back to the States.

I was discharged the next morning and a close friend of my mother's, someone I had known since I was a child, took me into her home. Noah's church members flooded the house with food. One of the local shops and several other people brought clothes and toiletries for my use.

The community was distraught. Not only had they lost a good friend—my mother—they had also lost their beloved pastor. Everyone was numb, going through the motions as they made their deliveries and expressed their condolences. I overheard someone say that Chrissy was receiving 24/7 care, and rightfully so. I could hear low whispers of how she was incoherent. Lost. Not eating. Not drinking enough water. Staying in bed. Sitting in a chair. Staring. Crying. Not talking. Not praying.

Oh, and the praying . . . People were praying all over the place. They prayed over me. They prayed over the food. They may have been praying over the furniture or the radio that provided background noise, including the breaking news and updates regarding the explosion that nearly leveled a home in North East, Maryland.

People were praying over everything.

Right. And where was God before the explosion?
And the firebombing had been carried out by one of his so-called righteous servants. Right?

Nigel and his family were under protective custody, moved to an undisclosed location, and the hunt was on for Carl Harper.

When Tyler and the girls finally arrived the day after the blast, I found the wherewithal to perk up. I was determined to put on a brave face in front of my young daughters. It was no secret that the Cuthbertson house had been fire bombed. Charlie and Maddie would surely hear about it. But, they needed to hear it from me first. I had to help them understand that there are bad people in this world.

Someone did not like the fact that my mother had offered her waterfront property as a place to baptize a young, gay man. I had to help my children understand that even though their grandmother was a wonderful person, there was someone out there who meant her harm.

And yes, I cried. My mother had died instantly in the blast. I was told that she didn't suffer and that she probably didn't know what had happened. Everyone said how lucky I was to have been down at the dock at the time. That "God was watching out for you."

If God was "watching out" at all, why didn't he protect my mother? Why didn't he stop this Carl Harper guy, whoever he is? Why did he allow Noah's life to be taken? Huh?

"Daddy said Grandmom went to heaven," Maddie, our youngest, stated. She was repeating what she had been told as a way to comfort me.

"Yes, she most definitely did."

"Daddy said she's all better now," Maddie continued.

"Yes, she is all better and probably very happy, too," I added.

Sitting on my lap, Maddie squirmed a little. It was a lot for her to take in. Living in Seattle and being so young, my girls didn't know my mother as well as I would have liked. They saw her once a year when we would make the trek back for a week's visit.

Charlie, I could sense, was focusing on "the bad people."

"Mom, is that bad person still around?" she asked, pushing her glasses back up onto the bridge of her little nose.

"No, Charlie. You don't need to worry about that bad person. He's in jail now. He can't hurt anyone anymore."

In the midst of all the surrounding sadness, funeral arrangements had to be made. Not only was there grieving to contend with, there was also the business of death. What was left of the house had to be combed through by my sister and me. The estate had to be settled, a slog that would continue for the next twelve months, or more, so we were told.

Both my mother and Noah were cremated. The day after Mom's well-attended memorial service and reception, Hope and I, along with her husband and my little family, gathered on the dock. There, we gently poured Mom's ashes into the river with the outgoing tide. Charlie and Maddie each threw a bouquet of pink carnations into the water and all of us watched as the flowers drifted away. When it was time to leave the dock, Tyler placed his arm around my shoulder and walked beside me while Charlie and Maddie scampered off ahead of us. Tyler called out, reminding them to stay away from the house—or what was left of it. As Tyler and I walked passed the boathouse, I looked up in time to peek through the window. A warm glow brought me unexpected comfort.

The following day, we attended Noah's "Celebration of Life." The small church was standing room only, but congregants had made sure that the six of us had seats up front. Chrissy, Noah's parents, and Thomas were greeting people as they came through the door and into the foyer. As I leaned in to give Chrissy a hug, she whispered into my ear.

"Can I see you before you leave for Seattle?"

"Yes . . . of course."

How much did she know?

I had no idea.

Mr. and Mrs. McKenna coldly shook my hand before I introduced Tyler, Charlie, Maddie, Hope, and Drew. Before moving on, Mrs. McKenna's eyes narrowed, sending me a warning shot.

Taking our seats, I was cognizant of the person who was missing her father's service: Janie.

She should be here. Noah would have wanted her here.

But, in truth, Noah was with her and I no longer needed to worry about Janie once I returned to Seattle. In momentary relief, I smirked. Then I chuckled. I bent my head and smiled into my hands so no one could see. I was balled over with joy and sadness swirling together like running a knife through two colors of icing on a cake. Noah was now with Janie. I was sure of it. They were going to be fine. Even his mother couldn't separate them now.

I gazed back at Chrissy who remained standing at the door. Indeed, she looked frail. While I would find comfort and strength with my husband and children, Chrissy would have to bear up under her grief. She was alone now. Her one and only was gone. Her in-laws would return to West Chester where they would continue to coddle Thomas, who was now standing beside them, a young man in his twenties.

The day after Noah's service, we were to take a late flight back to Seattle, giving me the morning and afternoon to go over some estate business with Hope, do some final packing, and see Chrissy as she had asked.

Walking up to her front stoop was like an out of body experience. Beyond that door was where Noah had spent most of his happiest moments in life. Beyond that door was the one person for whom he would have sacrificed everything. And beyond that door was the person who adored the man he had become.

I rang the doorbell and muffled chimes began singing inside the house. I could hear her footsteps approach, the turn of the lock, and then I was face to face with the one who had been left behind.

"Hi, Faith. Thanks for coming over. C'mon in."

"I hope this time is still OK?"

"Yes. This is perfect. I think this is the first time I've been alone since this all happened."

I had anticipated that we would hug each other, cry together, and commiserate in our misery. But that didn't happen. Chrissy, instead, escorted me right into the family room and waved me in the direction of a comfy chair.

"Would you like to have a seat? Some water or iced tea?"

"Water would be fine."

I studied the interior of the house while Chrissy disappeared into the nearby kitchen. Hanging on the opposite wall from where I was sitting was a large oil painting of verdant hills peppered with spring flowers. An old post and rail fence was prominent in the foreground and the blue sky above the scene came alive with cumulus clouds that cast moving shadows across the expansive rolling background. The artist's use of light and color resulted in creating dimensions that even a photographer would have been challenged to capture on film. I moved closer to see if I would recognize the signature. "C. McKenna." My hand covered my mouth to silence my gasp. Such talent. I had no idea she was an artist. There was so much I didn't know about this woman that Noah had clung to.

The room was small and the chairs were overstuffed, cramping the space somewhat. On the end table next me was a picture of Noah and Chrissy. Taken outside at some indiscriminate location, the two of them were seated upon a large rock, happily huddled together. They were wearing hiking gear and both were smiling with young love in their eyes.

Chrissy returned with two glasses of ice water, handing one over to me before sitting down on the other chair.

"Faith, I am so sorry about your mother. She was the dearest person on earth and she and Noah were thick as thieves."

"What?"

"Oh, Noah adored her."

"He did?"

"Yes. It was a mutual thing, I'm sure. I think he was like the son she never had."

"I guess I can see that?" I responded curiously.

Where is this headed?

"It's very evident that you and Noah, as well, had a special bond," she continued.

"Chrissy . . ."

"No, it's OK. Noah was a good man with a big heart," she sniffed and began choking up, tears dropping from her eyes and into her lap. "I'm sorry," she apologized, reaching for a tissue, "I didn't think I could cry anymore."

Her sadness touched me deeply. Without warning, I was in the midst of internalizing her grief, for I had loved him, too.

"He adored you, Chrissy. I knew it the very first time I met you."

"Yes . . . but he shared something special with you. Something beyond my reach. He'd been preoccupied ever since you arrived."

"Maybe it was because of Nigel . . . and his decision to go against the Board of Elders?"

"No. We'd been through those sticky situations before. We had discussed it and prayed about it at length. With you, it was much different. He was lost in a cloud somewhere. It was much deeper than church business. You were a matter of his heart."

"I'm sorry, Chrissy. I really don't know what to say."

"Did you love him?"

Her question rattled my very core. I had not anticipated her candid and rather blunt question.

"Yes, Noah and I *were* very close at one time."

. . . and maybe if things had turned out differently . . .

"But, Chrissy, I can assure you that he absolutely adored you. You were his world."

Chrissy stood and paced across the room. Turning to face me, I thought she might crumble.

"Truth is, Faith, I don't know what I'm going to do without him. He was everything to me. Yet, I had this feeling that he was leaving, even before . . . this. He was no longer sharing the details of his day, or his concerns, or much of anything with me. Even his prayers became shallow—superficial, almost. I knew he wasn't being open and honest with me, or God. It's hard to explain. It's just something that a soul mate can feel . . . a certain intuition. I was afraid he was distancing himself from me, from everyone . . . because of you."

"No. You're wrong . . ."

I stopped mid-sentence. I couldn't lie to her. And I couldn't tell her the truth either.

"Chrissy, he would have given you the world if he had it to give."

"I miss him." She buried her face in her hands. I'm not sure she heard me. "So much," she sputtered as she crumbled back into the chair.

How much time passed while we each sat in silent misery, I'm not sure.

"Chrissy . . ." I began hesitantly, "would you like to see him again?" I asked, fondling the sundial in the pocket of my jean jacket.

"Oh, I'd give anything to see him," she murmured fervently.

"Come down to the dock with me. Right now."

After she was on her way, I let go of her hand. I yelled back to her, reminding her that she had to smash the sundial when she arrived and before she was reunited with Noah.

"Promise me!" I yelled. "Promise me you'll smash it!" I cried.

I wailed as I walked away from the boathouse. I stood on the end of the dock, and within minutes, the light within the boathouse went dark. They were gone. I would never see them again.

Well, Noah had said that we would all see each other again, one day. That was the foundation of his faith. That's where he said he found his strength in his darkest hours.

CHRISSY

Sitting in my usual pew in church, I was suddenly captivated by a new visitor. A handsome man, someone I had met before, sat down in the pew directly in front of me. I reached over and gently tapped him on the shoulder.

"Hi! Chrissy Webber. Remember me? We met at the tavern?"

Noah turned in his seat and took my proffered hand.
"Yes, I do remember."
"Is this your first time here?"
"Yes. It's *our* first time here."

Right, I recalled. *He's married.*

"My daughter, Janie, should be along any second."
"I look forward to meeting her . . . and your wife."
"Um, well, my wife . . ."

At that moment, an older woman seated next to Noah spun around and glared at me.

"Uh . . . Chrissy, this is my mother-in-law, Mrs. Cuthbertson."

Fortunately, our awkward moment was interrupted by Noah McKenna's spitting image, a beautiful teenage girl with long, vibrant hair and wide crystal blue eyes. She looked concerned . . . and somewhat melancholy, a contradiction of her physical beauty.

"Grandmom, why did you sit so far down front?"

The older woman didn't respond. She turned back toward the front of the church.

"I'm not sure why we sat here," Noah lamented. "Janie, this is Miss Chrissy Webber."

"Nice to meet you, Miss Webber," Janie replied, as she obviously had been taught to do.

I waited for Noah's wife to join them, but she never appeared.

As we sang the closing hymn, "God Be With You 'Til We Meet Again," I noticed Noah slip his arm around his daughter's shoulder and she held on tight to his waist. They were sharing a moment. A very wounded and tender moment.

After the service, outside, a middle-aged woman approached me. I must have been staring at Noah, or something. Anyway, the woman leaned in and whispered, "His wife passed away in a freak accident. Just days ago. That place that was struck by lightning? Belongs to his mother-in-law, the woman that was sitting beside him. Anyway, sometime after the blast, when everyone was gone, his wife had gone back to the property to retrieve something from the boathouse. Word has it that she fell into the river and broke her neck. Poor man. I've heard that he's been there every day since, at low tide, searching for something that belonged to them. A shell, of all things."

AUTHOR'S NOTE

Writing this novel has been very cathartic for me. I have always been a person who dwelled on the "what ifs" of my life. After our daughter, Jamie, died in a car accident, the "what ifs" surrounding her death plagued me, further convincing me that I was at fault for something that—I now realize—was completely out of my control.

This fictional story became a way for me to journal through my thoughts. It has helped me realize that if we knew the answers to all of our "what ifs," the answers, themselves, would only lead us toward more conjecture, and on and on. Therefore, I have concluded that our suppositions about the past are best left in the past.

The ability to navigate all of the possible outcomes of a given hypothetical situation is a blessing for the risk manager or the trouble-shooter. However, living in the "what ifs" of our pasts, can be a real curse especially after a devastating, life-changing event. It can become all-consuming. It is downright unhealthy.

If not in the car accident, it is very possible that Jamie may have predeceased us in some other way. But I have no way of knowing. However, there is one thing I am sure of: We will see her again and what a joyful reunion that will be!

Perhaps my greatest revelation was that no matter what road a person chooses to travel, the ending will always turn out to be the same, only the scenic paths and the challenges faced during the journey are different. Our arrival times may vary, too. Regardless, we will manage to get there, eventually.

Be kind to yourselves. Hold on to the happy memories and look ahead. Every day is another day closer. There are happy reunions awaiting us. Conclusive answers will come soon enough.

If you enjoyed **"Sundial,"** consider reading other novels written by Jill Hicks.

From the popular "Bay Avenue" series:
"BAY AVENUE: The Inheritance"

is the story of three brothers and their connection to a beach house in the quaint shore town of Lewes, Delaware. The house had been in the family for generations when a beautiful redhead and an unexpected relative entered their lives. Romance and power struggles become a heartbreaking combination, changing family dynamics forever.

"BAY AVENUE II: The Courtship"

finds an attractive Lewes, Delaware attorney dealing with the pain of unrequited love compounded by her own destructive insecurities. Often the outsider-looking-in, she painfully learns to overcome life's scars.

"BAY AVENUE III: Pratt-ically Speaking,"

finds three young couples struggling to survive the choices they have made and the hands they have been dealt. Life isn't fair. Love can be complicated. Not all endings are happily ever after, or are they?

"The Long Climb Back"

is the story of an adventurous young woman who strikes out on her own after an over-the-top marriage proposal from a winery heir. Her travels introduce her to two engaging brothers. Will she be able to return to her fiancé with her mind, body, and soul intact?

"Adrift"

follows the journey of Carly Young Mariner, a devoted wife, mother, and second grade teacher, who walks in on an encounter that upends her ordinary life. Overtime—but not out of time—she distances herself from her family and everything that has given her a sense of purpose. With hope of finding contentment and a place to contemplate her options, Carly escapes to the Outer Banks of North Carolina. Shortly after her arrival, a minor accident transforms her and those around her.

ACKNOWLEDGEMENTS

My deepest gratitude is always reserved for my very patient and loving husband, Bill. He encourages me and "markets" my books whenever the opportunity arises. Bill has provided the cover photos and layouts for all of my novels, but this one may be my favorite thus far. I don't believe I would have ventured into independent writing without his support and advocacy.

This book would not have been possible without my parents for obvious reasons; however, it was their love of boating that has inspired much of my writing. My parents owned a boat throughout my childhood. Every summer weekend, weather permitting, we were on a boat that they had kept docked at Bay Boat Works in North East, Maryland. I know the North East River like the back of my hand. I have waterskied its entire length, crabbed off Turkey Point, and tacked back and forth across its busy channel in a sailboat many times. Bay Boat Works is the setting of many happy memories for me.

My deepest thanks and fondest love goes to Peggy Kratz and her mother, Nancy Kratz. Peggy and I have been close friends since high school. Her parents also owned a boat docked at Bay Boat Works, as well as a beautiful piece of property on the North East River, not far from the setting of this book. Growing up on this river and spending time at the Kratz "cabin," inspired many of my descriptive recollections of the area during the time of this story. While in the editing process, Peggy and I hiked out to the Turkey Point Lighthouse to insure that I had accurately captured the ambiance of the area. During this trip, Peggy also introduced me to an old and little known cemetery that is tucked away off the beaten path. The surnames of its "residents," from the eighteenth and nineteenth centuries, inspired the surnames of this story's main characters.

Next, I need to thank my sister, Jane, and her husband, Mike, a.k.a. "Monkey Mike." We have shared many travels and laughs over the years. It is usually during one of these trips that my stories take flight. Jane has always been kind enough to read and provide edits, especially pointing out any inconsistencies. She has saved me from some embarrassing chronological discrepancies.

My sister, Joan, has also been instrumental in the initial stages of editing. Throughout life, she has accepted no less than the best from herself and those around her. Knowing that she would demand excellence if given this project, I asked her to take her best shot. She always catches errors of all kinds. Thanks, Joan!

Edna Spath and Sharon Ruscansky blessed me not only with edits, they also gave me a gift. While in the midst of the tedious editing process, Bill and I took a trip to Florida, where we met up with the Spaths and Ruscanskys in Placida. The six of us went to the Sandbar Tiki & Grille to have dinner and watch the sunset over the Gulf. That evening the outdoor restaurant hosted a live band that was made up of some phenomenal musicians. It just so happens that it would have been our daughter's thirty-third birthday. The first song the band played? "Isn't She Lovely," by Stevie Wonder, a song that Bill and I would sing to Jamie when she was an infant. Unbeknownst to anyone, I had spent the day wondering if Jamie could really be with me everywhere I traveled. Her spirit stirred within me in ways I cannot put into words. A surge of sheer joy brought tears to my eyes, which I hid from everyone. Thanks, Edna and Sharon, for the time you took to edit this book, and for blessing me in such a profound way.

My deep appreciation and gratitude goes to my editor, Ralph Painter, who offers me hours of his time not only to edit, but most importantly, to mentor me. I have enjoyed and cherished the instruction he has provided: explaining best writing practices, grammatical corrections, and suggested techniques. Never in a million years would I ever believe that writing could be so fascinating, until I met Ralph and he began sharing his wealth of knowledge and experience with me. Ralph, you have given me the confidence to continue my pursuit of literary expression.

Most of all, I need to thank my readers, especially those who have written reviews, forwarded their comments, have invited me into their homes to attend their book clubs, have attended my book signing events, or have joined my Facebook page, "Jill Hicks–Author." What a great experience it has been for me to hear what you thought and felt as you traveled through these pages with me. Thank you for your encouragement, it means the world to me.

Thank you for joining me in this most unexpected journey.

Blessings, Jill

ABOUT THE AUTHOR

Jill L Hicks was born and raised in West Chester, Pennsylvania, and currently resides in Lewes, Delaware, with her husband, Bill. Together, they have two daughters. Tragically, they lost their first, Jamie, in an auto accident when she was just twenty. Jamie is survived by her younger sister, Jessie, and her half-sister, Jenn.

Jill is very close to her extended family. She draws on her personal experiences and the stories of others to express the joys and sorrows of life and love.

Jill is a graduate of Penn State University with a degree in Music Education. In her spare time she enjoys boating, playing the piano, reading, cycling, and spending quality beach time with her husband, family, and friends.

Ironically, Jill loathed reading until just several years ago. Suddenly, poring through twenty to thirty books a year, she ran out of books to read and decided to write her own, ergo her first novel, "BAY AVENUE: The Inheritance."

Made in the USA
Columbia, SC
15 June 2018